Brenna Lyons

Matchmaker's Misery

Kegin Series #3

FIREBORN PUBLISHING COPYRIGHT

STATEMENT

Matchmaker's Misery
Copyright © 2005/5009/2017 by Brenna Lyons
Print ISBN: 978-1-946004-85-7
Print Publication: March 2017

Cover Artist: Brenna Lyons
Photo Credit: 123rf
Logo copyright © 2014 by Fireborn Publishing and
Allison Cassatta
Licensed material is being used for illustrative
purposes only. Any person depicted in the
licensed material is a model.

sales@firebornpublishing.com or via the author's personal email.

All characters and events in this book are fictitious. Any resemblance to actual persons, living or dead, is strictly coincidental.

This book is written in US English.

PUBLISHER

Glossary of Keen Terms

Used in the Book

NOTE: Keen is a lyrical language, and minor changes in pitch and inflection denote a slightly different word in the language. See next page for the Keen calendar.

Assurances— the presentation of a bloodied blade to an injured woman, offering proof that the guilty party has faced his punishment at your hand; assurances are usually offered by a noble or royal husband, father, adult brother or a noble or royal executioner

Cimmeg— a heavy spice like cinnamon and vanilla mixed that strengthens the blood and aids in healing

Dolgen— a yellow/orange scrubby plant which yields a powerful aphrodisiac; sucre sweet, it can be ingested in a tea; for the most powerful and immediate potency, it is mixed in oil and applied to genitalia

Fion— Keen queen of the gods; Goddess of love, balance and mercy

Fion's Children/Daughters— the matriarchal priestess race wiped out by the Lengar in Ti 10-452

Garigol— a powerful sedative and muscle relaxant derived from the leaves and nectar of the tree of the same name; causes confusion and lethargy followed by sleep, in higher doses; Jaglin crave it and will attack to steal stores of it, so it is stored in air-tight containers

Geela— a cliff-diving, carrion eating bird with gray and black feathers

Gelgrin— a confection made of Eir sap, lizor berries, implin, and cream

Hi— the formal address for a Keen prince, Your/His Highness

Hir— the formal address for a Keen princess, Your/Her Highness

Hitem— the formal address for a couple or group of princes/princesses or a mix of the two, Your/His/Her Highnesses

Implin— a Keen fruit akin to a Bosc pear; the core is a strong stimulant; the main ingredient in lover's repast

Iri— golden flowers that grow on vines as thick as a man's wrist; makes a soothing topical drug for use on rashes, minor burns and abrasions; makes a strong liquor

Kit— breeding cattle, which are used for food

Kittle— a small, furry domestic animal like a cross between a kitten and a rabbit

Laes— the formal address for a Keen noblewoman

Len— God of the underworld, vows broken, trickery and havoc

Li— the formal address for a Keen nobleman

Lizor— a fragrant purple flower whose berries make a calming tea; the stems make a powerful sedative to relax the mind and body; lizor is also used in forming a healing circle

Lover's Repast— the traditional cake of new lovers and new mothers; Cimmeg and Implin cakes with warmed sucre sap served on the side

Mag— Keen king of the gods; God of justice, law and vows unbroken

Magden— the race ruled by Ro Ti in the days before unification

Olum— a drug like an opiate that relaxes muscles, relieves pain and suppresses the drive to vomit

Oxykol— a toxin formed during a Keen pregnancy; it causes the pregnancy signs; when left unchecked, the toxins will incapacitate and ultimately kill the sufferer

Ri— the formal address for a Keen king, Your/His Majesty

Rig— the formal address for a Keen queen, Your/Her Majesty

Rihem— the formal address for the royal couple, Your Majesties

Schaen— a male harem, kept for the use of royal females; named for the schen

Schen— the insatiable sex drive of a pregnant Keen woman

Schente— a harem of sterilized women, kept for the use of royal men

Silin— a silk-like fabric that most women's clothing and royal bedding are made from

Sivrah— a Gypsy-like race of matriarchal Keen who work as migrant field hands, travel in family caravans of living transports and live largely outside the governance of Keen law

Stride— a measure of distance: the distance the average war-buck can travel at a loping stride (half-speed) in the space of five minutes; a speed of hottel travel: full stride is full speed and half-stride is a comfortable loping speed

Sucre— a thick sugar syrup from Eir trees

Trial Moon— an ancient custom by which a Keen man may demand a contract by a woman he has had sex with if certain conditions are met

Zura— a gray bush, used in protection oils for blessing and healing circles; makes a tonic when mixed with Garigol that eases painful breathing

KEEN CALENDAR

A year on Kegin is roughly equivalent to an Earth year. Days are twenty Earth hours long, but the year is separated into twelve months consisting of thirty-seven days each. A week on Kegin consists of eight of their days. I formatted the calendar as if the Keen year started in January like an Earth year. In reality, the Keen year begins in Endl. The end of winter and beginning of spring is a time of rebirth, and so it is the start of the Keen New Year.

Pri— January
Ite— February
Endl— March
Wos— April
Zor— May
Fim— June
Jad— July
Caj— August
Wend— September
Abrin— October
Veril— November
Iric— December

THE MAJOR RE-BRED FAMILIES

OF KEGIN

Kell and Jenneane (Last Chance For Love 1):
Jole (Susan - Last Chance For Love 1)
Michael (Danellan - Last Chance For Love 1)

Jole and Susan:
Jenneane (Tirin - Rites of Mating 2)
Joseph (Berel - Rites of Mating 2)
Eve (Jearsen- Matchmaker's Misery 3)
Rebecca (Restrained 5)
Pyter (Restrained 5)

Michael and Danellan:
Gibril (Double Image 4)
Cro (Alien Encounters 6)
Kyra (Steden- Matchmaker's Misery 3)
Gandl (Restrained 5)
Dirin (Double Image 4)

Alex The Elder and Lyssa Braeden (Last Chance For Love 1):
Alex The Younger (Double Image 4)
Andrew (Double Image 4)
Pilar (Cored- Matchmaker's Misery 3)
Carter (Alien Encounters 6)

Jace and Jelise (In Her Ladyship's Service 1.5):
Cayce (Tale of Three Daughters 7)
Kylee (Tale of Three Daughters 7)
Kristee (Tale of Three Daughters 7)

NOTE TO THE READERS:

Welcome to the continuing Kegin series. My apologies for the long delay between the first few books and the rest. As I noted in RITES OF MATING, writing this series means writing large portions of every book initially, since all of the characters are so interwoven.

In addition, despite all of my scrupulous back-ups, a hard drive failure took the original final manuscript of MATCHMAKER'S MISERY. To my dismay, that meant typing in more than half of the book from the hand-written notes a second time, reconstituting 14,000 words of work that I'd typed into the computer directly—something I rarely do—and doing cleaning edits on the book a second time.

Thankfully, I don't expect those sorts of problems to occur again.

Thanks for your patience, and welcome back to Kegin! Remember, as always, there's a glossary and calendar, for your use.

Live honorably, love completely and laugh at life!
Brenna Lyons

Dedicated to...

Tamer, for putting up with long hours, deadlines, and noisy characters.

SECTION ONE:
Cored

The Stud

CHAPTER ⊕NE

Jad 10, Ri 25-3016

Pilar shivered, looking around for the man who'd touched her back, but no one seemed close enough to have been the one.

"*Anything wrong?*" Andrew asked in English, his chest pressed to her shoulder in a possessive manner any of the hopefuls would be sure to recognize.

She sank further into him. "*I thought...*" But the more she thought about it, the more ridiculous it sounded.

"*What?*" His voice was gruff, and her hair stirred at the movement of his head as he scanned the room.

"*Nothing.*" She laughed nervously. "*My imagination.*"

"*If you're certain...*" Andrew's voice announced clearly that he wasn't.

"*I—I am. I'm just being silly.*"

"*I'll stay with you.*"

Pilar turned to him, wincing at his open challenge to a group of hopefuls milling nearby. "*Please, Andrew. I'm fine. Really, I am.*"

"*If you're uneasy, you don't have to do this. I can escort you to your rooms.*"

Her cheeks heated. "*No. I'll never find a mate if you hover. I want to, Andrew. Promise me you'll let me try.*" Of course, she'd been trying for nearly a year, and she was still skittish as a kittle around the hopefuls.

He nodded, stroking at her cheek lightly. "*If you need my help—*"

Pilar smiled. "*I'm never alone.*"

Andrew dropped a kiss on her cheek, then withdrew. Pilar took a calming breath and smiled at the lord approaching her. She could do this. She could find a mate.

"Good evening, mi'lord," she offered brightly, searching for his name and coming up short...again. It was Lor...something, she was certain. It was deplorable that she couldn't remember most of their names. Then again, she'd only been actively meeting the nobles at events, and there were so many hopefuls at each one.

He bowed, keeping his eyes averted. "Good evening, Pilar Laes. Would you care to take some air with me?"

She stared at him in surprise. No man had dared ask her that in all the time she'd met men. "Why...yes, mi'lord. I believe I would," she managed.

Her heart skipped as the lord offered his arm. Pilar placed her hand through his elbow, glancing around for Andrew automatically. He was engaged in conversation with his twin, Alex. Their father and mother were dancing together, and Carter was nowhere in sight.

Pilar fought back a moment of panic. She was walking away with this lord, and none of her family would be trailing in her wake. Pilar straightened her spine and managed a smile for her escort. If she ever wanted to find a mate, it was the price she would have to pay.

The night air was cool and the stars bright. Pilar resisted the urge to laugh out loud. Like Carter, she'd always favored a clear, night sky.

"This is to your liking?" the man at her side asked.

"Yes. It is...Li..." Pilar grimaced in the realization that she still hadn't remembered his name. Was it Lorent? Lorel?

He chuckled. "Loryol, Pilar Laes."

Her cheeks burned in a fierce blush. "Loryol. Of course. My apologies, Loryol Li."

"None needed. You meet many men. You can hardly be expected to remember every name." Loryol met her eyes fully. "But, perhaps the most important are remembered...fondly remembered."

Pilar released his arm, suddenly uncertain. Something in Loryol's eyes was too familiar. She hadn't given him permission to look her in the eye, but he was doing so without hesitation.

She took a step toward the manor. "We should go back. My brothers—"

Loryol's hands closed on her shoulders, pulling Pilar into the shelter of his body. "Just a few moments," he requested.

"You—you don't have permission to touch me." Pilar's heart pounded in fear. She didn't want to scream, but Loryol might leave her no choice but to alert the guards.

"I mean you no harm." His voice was smooth...melodic.

"The law doesn't say—"

His lips brushed across hers. Pilar stiffened in surprise, pushing at Loryol's chest. His mouth came down again, bypassing her face and laying a kiss at her pulse point.

She stilled, her thoughts scattered. Loryol traced the artery with the tip of his tongue.

"You should stop," Pilar managed, her eyes sliding shut in the cascade of new stimuli.

She knew what Loryol was doing, of course. All the re-breds had been trained in Keen lovemaking. The women healers had told Pilar it was for her own protection. She'd never understood that comment until now.

Loryol's hand stroked at her hip, sending sparks of pleasure through her system. Pilar's mind worked dully at the situation. He was trying to seduce her. If Loryol succeeded, he could demand a Trial Moon.

"No." Pilar pushed him away more forcefully, trying to bolt for the manor.

His hand closed on her wrist, tighter than she was comfortable with, wrenching her back to him. Loryol's eyes glittered in the starlight, a fierce determination etched on his face.

"Release me," she ordered him, but her voice was devoid of the conviction she wanted it to carry.

"You should not play with a Keen lord," he informed her.

"I'm not playing. I'm leaving." Pilar pulled at his hold, her breathing hitching when he didn't budge. She looked toward the manor through the thick foliage hiding all but the highest windows from view, praying for some sound indicating that

Andrew was in pursuit. Even Carter would be acceptable at this point.

Loryol's grip tightened, a silent promise that she was going nowhere he didn't want her to go. He shook his head slowly. "Why do you fear me? Have I injured you?"

"If you don't release me—"

"Release her. Now."

Pilar jumped at the strange voice. She searched out the dark shadow moving toward them in relief. She wasn't alone and at Loryol's mercy.

"I said release her. I won't say it a third time."

She had a face to match to the voice now. Bathed in starlight, the fury of his words couldn't compare to the promise of death in his eyes.

Loryol chuckled. "Amazing. You actually think you can order me?"

"I can stop you, but I promise you that Alex Li the Elder and the lady's brothers will kill you where you stand if you don't release her. I'll make sure of it."

Loryol's cocky grin disappeared. He released her arm.

All of her life, Pilar had been trained to run to her family or guards in a case like this. She didn't. The moment she was free of Loryol, Pilar surged behind her savior.

He looked around at her in shock, then turned to Loryol. "Do you wish me to deliver Loryol to your father?" he asked solemnly.

Pilar shuddered, pressing her cheek to the man's back, his silin shirt soothing her nerves.

"No," she whispered. "My father knows where to find him."

"Very well."

Loryol stomped away, grumbling curses.

The second man stood his ground for several minutes. Finally, he sighed and relaxed slightly. "Are you well, Pilar Laes?"

She nodded against his back.

"Then I should take you to your—"

"Not yet...please." Pilar managed an unwavering voice though tears threatened.

He turned to her, his dark eyes growing darker in concern. His gaze scanned over her, boldly drinking in every inch of her body. "Were you hurt?"

"No," she denied, though she rubbed at her wrist. She did hurt, and Andrew's fury wasn't something Pilar wanted to see anytime soon.

The man scooped up her hand, his eyes narrowing. "I should have taken him to your father. We should go now. They can stop Loryol before—"

"No," she gasped. There had to be a better way. Seeing Pilar come in with a mark on her body would send Andrew over the edge of reason. "Alex," she mused. If Alex healed the bruise, before Andrew saw it...

"Pardon?"

"If you brought my brother Alex— Oh... No. You won't know which is which," she decided miserably.

"Does it matter?"

"Of course, it does," she snapped. "If Alex heals this before Andrew sees—"

"You want to heal the damage before you go in?"

"Unless I want to be under heavy guard for the rest of my life." That wasn't a stretch of the imagination. She'd never find a mate that way. "But, how will you tell them apart?"

"I don't need to," he offered in a voice that sounded of complete confidence in his answer.

"Yes, you do need to. Or...someone needs to." Who could he ask, without arousing suspicion? *Carter!* Her younger brother bordered on oblivious.

"If healing is the problem, let me heal you."

Pilar stared at him, shocked beyond speech for an instant, but the young lord seemed sincere. "You possess the healing magic?"

He raised an eyebrow, as if frustrated by the question. "Yes. I do." His tone rode the line between patient and patronizing.

"But...it's so rare. The royal family and the re-breds, naturally. Other than that, there are only...perhaps...a dozen men—"

"Fifteen, to be precise," he offered with a slight tip of his head.

"How wonderful." Pilar touched his arm, feeling like a silly school girl in his presence. "A treasure," she breathed.

"Pardon?" he asked again.

"My apologies. I meant... You're a treasure."

"My healing magic?" he scoffed.

"And your noble nature. Not every man would have stopped Loryol. Many men would have taken advantage of the situation, if they'd done anything at all."

He blushed. "May I heal you?"

"Absolutely." She offered her arm, her heart skipping in excitement. She'd never been healed by anyone but her immediate family and her Cousin Joseph. "With my thanks."

The lord cradled her wrist to his mouth and started to heal the bruises.

Pilar weaved on her feet in surprise. The healing was always enjoyable, but coming from an eligible young lord instead of a family member made it more so.

The sensation of ice hit her first. Then the heat, followed closely by the pulse of pleasure. Her human genetics made this simple exchange more erotic than the seduction attempts Loryol had played at.

Pulse after pulse of his healing coursed over her nerves, bringing her nipples to aching points against her gown, making her sex hot and heavy and her thighs damp with the lubricant for lovemaking.

The lord placed a kiss on the inside of her wrist, marking the end of his healing.

"What is your name?" Pilar asked, her voice strange in her own ears.

He met her gaze, seemingly surprised. "Cored, mi'lady."

She nodded shakily. "Cored Li," she greeted him, rising on her toes and sealing her mouth to his.

* * * *

Cored groaned in surprise, drinking in the musk on her skin and the press of her nipples through both layers of silin between them. Len only knew why, but Pilar was aroused. His inner sense told him that she was intent on him, on taking Cored in the garden, if he'd have her.

This is a bad idea, his mind protested. *Take her to her father. Do this the right way. She wants you. You could be contracted within the week.*

His mind was drowned out by the flood of emotions his sense pulled from Pilar. Her need was like a living thing. With his reputation—the little of it his brother had allowed to leak out, at risk to the family—her manic sexual state could be blamed on Cored's failings.

Some dark corner of his mind produced a new plan. Pilar had initiated this encounter. If she followed it through, Cored could demand a Trial Moon.

Pilar pulled at his tunic, frantic, her musk reaching a high that indicated a mating frenzy in full sway. Her mouth parted from his. "Cored," she pleaded.

"You want this?" he whispered. She had to say it.

"Yes." She pulled at the buttons on his trousers, opening them and taking his length in her hand.

Cored shivered, cupping her face up and meeting her mouth, letting her need feed his own. He lowered her to the ground, pulling up at her full skirts.

She was ready for him, her heated body slick. Pilar bowed up to his questing fingers, her eyes wide. Cored groaned in pleasure as he encountered her barrier.

Slowly, he reminded himself. Cored sought out the ridge of her inner pleasure spot.

Pilar was responsive. She moved against his hands, sharp gasps and low moans escaping her trembling lips.

At the moment of her climax, Cored captured her cry in his mouth. It was necessary. A scream would bring her father and brothers.

Pilar fixed pleading eyes on him. Cored nodded. He didn't need to ask the ritual words; Cored could feel exactly what Pilar wanted, but there was something beyond arousal that Cored wished he had the time to examine...something he hadn't encountered before.

Cored sealed his lips to hers again, seating his cock deep inside her. Her climax quickened as Pilar's barrier tore, and her arousal grew. To his surprise, she didn't cry out.

The swell of unrecognized feelings grew, and Cored opened himself to them more fully. The realization of what she was feeling jarred him. Pilar trusted him. She liked him...perhaps more than liked him.

Other women he'd bedded wanted something from him, harbored ulterior motives that brought the sour taste of mercenary emotions to the forefront of their hearts. None of them had trusted him. Few liked him, and none liked him more than what they wanted from him.

He touched her face, guilt coursing through him. It shocked him...appalled him on some base level. Cored hadn't bargained on this. He hadn't anticipated feeling anything in response to her emotions, but he did.

I didn't expect her emotions to be so positive and warm.

Cored slowed his pace, taking Pilar in long, leisurely strokes, reveling in her heated reactions. He groaned. Maybe their contract wouldn't be a sham, after all.

* * * *

Andrew jumped up on the dais, scanning the ballroom for some sign of Pilar. She was gone. He jumped down again and strode toward Carter. Since Andrew had been with Alex, Carter was his only hope for information.

He ground his teeth in frustration. It wasn't like Pilar to disappear like this. That, coupled with her unease earlier in the evening, spoke volumes to Andrew.

"Carter," he barked at his younger brother. "Where is Pilar?"

"In the gardens," he answered automatically.

Andrew breathed a sigh of relief. "Where?"

Carter shot him a look of disbelief. "Does it look like I followed them?"

The unease returned like a punch to his gut. "Them? Who was with her?"

"Some lord. Um... Loral, I think. No... Loryol. That's it."

"You think? Carter, are you telling me that you let Pilar walk out there with a notorious rake and no guard?"

"She's an adult, Andrew. *For Pete's sake!* What she does is none of my business."

"It is. Protecting Pilar is our duty. How long ago did they leave the ballroom?"

Carter shrugged. "A quarter of an hour. Maybe a half."

Andrew grasped his shoulder. "A quarter or a half?" he demanded.

Carter shrugged again.

Andrew uttered several harsh curses in English and Keen. "Stay here in case Pilar comes back."

His younger brother rolled his eyes, but he nodded his agreement.

Andrew collected Alex and two of the guards, heading out into the night.

"Which way, Andrew Li?" the lieutenant asked.

Andrew scanned his eyes over the expansive gardens in dismay. "We'll have to split up."

"I don't think so," Alex commented, his voice tenser than usual. He marched down the hillside before Andrew could question his certainty.

Andrew followed his brother's line of sight, and his gaze settled on Loryol emerging from the Garigol trees...alone. Alex made it to Loryol first, but only by a moment.

"Where is she?" Alex demanded.

Loryol scowled then motioned into the trees. "Back there. Believe me, she's fine."

Andrew took over. "Why did you leave her? Why are you heading to the transports instead of the manor?"

"Because your sister seems to prefer the company of others. If you'll excuse me—" He turned and made to push past the guards.

"Stop him," Alex ordered.

Loryol looked back in something approaching fury. "All I did was try to talk to her."

"*All* you did?" Andrew drawled. "Are you certain about that?" Loryol was too defensive, too cocky. Something more had happened, Andrew was sure.

Loryol shifted uncomfortably, his face darkening, confirming that Andrew was correct. "Well...I did kiss her, I suppose. But she was willing," he was quick to add. "More than willing, and I did stop when she requested that I stop. You've got no reason to hold me."

"I think we do. Until I hear the same story from Pilar's lips, I think you should remain a guest of the house. Lieutenant?"

"As you wish," the guard replied, shooting Loryol a look of warning.

"Now," Alex began calmly. "Where is my sister?"

Loryol sighed. "Last time I saw her, she was hanging all over him near a stand of flowering Zura bushes."

"All over who?" Alex's voice held more than a touch of acid.

"Cored." Loryol managed a stiff smile. "What a lovely judge of character your sister is."

Andrew headed into the gardens at a near run, stopping several times to get his bearings.

Cored. Loryol hadn't called him Cored Li for a reason. Cored had been disavowed by his family. Andrew didn't know why he'd been, but he knew Cored was considered a dangerous man. Only his affiliations allowed him entry to estates like this

13

one. It seemed many of the noble families tolerated, even invited his attendance at events.

Alex tapped him on the shoulder, reminding Andrew that he was about to miss the path to the stand of Zura. They turned together, picking their way up the less-used path.

"Cored."

Andrew stilled in disbelief at the passionate whisper. *I don't want to see this.* Whatever was going on, he was sure it wasn't good.

Pilar groaned. "Cored."

It definitely wasn't getting better. Slight sounds of movement sent a shiver of dread down Andrew's spine.

Alex grasped his shoulder, stepping ahead of his younger twin and heading into the bushes separating them from the couple beyond. Of course, Alex had probably become jaded to the idea of sex, younger sister or not.

A masculine groan sent Andrew into motion again. "My Pilar," Cored crooned.

Alex stopped short, shaking his head as if in denial of what he was seeing. Andrew shouldered him aside, his breath catching at the scene in the clearing.

Pilar lay beneath Cored, her gold silin gown pushed to her waist, her legs hooked around his waist. Cored's fingers were threaded through hers, pressing Pilar's hands to the ground to either side of her head. He laid kiss after kiss on her lips, whispering endearments to her between, capturing little gasps and moans from her swollen lips. He moved inside her, his cock appearing and disappearing into her trembling body.

"Yes, Cored," she pleaded, her body rising against his, the scent of her climax perfuming the air in the small clearing and rushing past her brothers on air currents.

Cored nodded, slamming his body deep into hers, his head thrown back, his eyes closing in a look of bliss.

Alex surged toward them, gleaning the meaning of that move a split-second before Andrew did. Pilar's cry of delight dissolved into dismay as Alex grasped Cored by the throat and dragged him off of her, his erupting cock spraying thick rivulets of his seed along her thighs and over the dark blonde curls at the apex. Cored released her hands at the drag of her body along with him, letting her thump softly to the grass.

Cored roared in pain and frustration, his thickening cock far from the band he sought. He collapsed to his bare backside, dragging Alex with him, his eyes wide and body trembling in shock.

"No," Pilar sobbed, one hand reaching for him in a slow, unsteady arc.

Andrew knelt at her side, trying to soothe her upset. She was in a mating frenzy. Pilar didn't understand what Cored's game was.

"How could you?" she accused, her midnight blue eyes full of tears.

Andrew sighed, drawing her skirts down her abdomen. He closed his eyes to the sight of Cored's seed leaking from her body, a trickle of blood mixed in, probably the evidence of her barrier. He prayed that's all it was.

"Was this the first?" he started to ask.

Pilar slapped his cheek, forcing his eyes open to the sight of the tears streaming down her face.

"How could you!" she repeated, struggling to her feet. Pilar sank to her knees with a gasp, pressing a hand to her abdomen, pale and shaking.

Andrew turned on Cored, laying a punch across his cheek that sent the disavowed lord into Alex's chest and nearly overbalanced them both.

"Stop," Alex ordered. "You don't know what happened here."

"Don't I?"

Cored shook his head, but whether it was a mute protest or to clear the ringing residue of the punch was unclear.

"No. You don't know...not for certain. Leave him, until Pilar is capable of telling us."

Andrew nodded, drawing Pilar into his arms.

She smacked him again, this time with enough power behind it to make Andrew see bright flashes of light in its wake. "Don't touch me," she growled at him. "I hate you."

He nodded; in the midst of a mating frenzy, no matter the situation, Pilar would strike out at anyone who'd interrupted her. "Alex, bring that geela with you. I'll get Pilar to the woman healer."

CHAPTER TWO

Cored moved his wrists to a more comfortable position within the shackles, casting a nervous glance at his row of irate judges. He'd known it had been a bad idea; he should have taken his own counsel on that. He'd argued it with himself.

And the idiot in the argument won. I should have taken her to her father and taken my chances.

His cock still ached from the abrupt end to their coitus. Keen men weren't designed for a shock like that. The brother—*Alex*, he would guess... Pilar said Alex was the calmer of the two. Alex couldn't have hurt Cored more if he'd planned the move in advance. Even Andrew's blow hadn't hurt as much as that withdrawal.

Cored sobered. Andrew's blow hadn't hurt as much as seeing the young lord carry Pilar away from him, as if Cored meant to harm her.

He shifted uneasily. Keen women weren't designed for the shock they'd suffered, either...especially when it was a first mating. He'd been too muddled in his own pain to consider the depth of hers earlier, but now that he had, it was hard to think of much else. Even the shackles he wore seemed to dim into the background of his mind.

The door opened, and Lyssa Laes entered. Cored lowered his gaze respectfully. He hadn't forgotten all civility, after all.

"How is she?" Andrew asked urgently.

"Furious," his mother replied. "Your sister may never forgive you for this."

Andrew blanched at that determination. "The pain? The blood?" he continued. Was he seeking a reason to kill Cored or just assuring himself that Pilar was well?

"Interrupting a Keen first mating is dangerous, Andrew. Pilar's body was prepared for completion, and you two—"

"It was that or—" Andrew stopped short, looking at the door in disbelief as Pilar ambled in, wrapped in a silin robe.

"Gods, Pilar," Andrew complained, dragging his uniform jacket down his arms and crossing the room toward her.

She glared at him, raising a single pointing finger in warning. "Don't even *think* about touching me."

"You're not dressed," her father reminded her.

"And everyone in this room has seen me this far undressed or further," she challenged.

The Earth-born Alex Li darkened, his mouth working as if to protest. His bride stifled a laugh, and Carter laughed outright. Alex the younger covered his mouth, as if hiding a smile. Andrew looked unimpressed with his sister's observation.

Cored swallowed a blast of laughter at the tapestry of responses, meeting Pilar's eyes as she turned to him.

She offered him a smile. It faded at the sight of his shackled hands. Pilar turned on her older brothers. "Release him," she demanded.

Alex and Andrew shared a look of consideration. Alex shrugged as if in answer to some comment his twin had made, then leaned back against his father's desk. Andrew crossed his arms over his chest and stared down at her.

"Now, Andrew. I mean it. You've taken this too far."

He didn't move to comply.

Pilar stormed across the room and started searching his pockets for the lock bar. Cored considered telling her that Alex the younger had it but decided that might annoy his judges further. It was probably better to stay silent.

Andrew grasped at her wrists and forced them back, and Cored tensed in response. If her brother made one move that might injure her, all wagers and plans were abandoned. He'd fought in shackles before, and he could do so again. It wasn't civilized, but Cored wasn't part of polite society anymore. Cullin had made certain of that.

"When I'm satisfied he's not at fault," Andrew replied brusquely, "and not before."

She swiveled her head to appeal to her parents. "Maum? Dahd?"

Cored sent a look of supplication skyward. *Oh no. They can't switch to English now.* He cursed himself silently for not taking the time to learn their primary language. It would have meant selling his genetics another time or two, but it would have been worth it.

Alex the elder shook his head, adopting the same cross-armed stance his middle son had taken. "When we're through."

Pilar started to motion to her mother, but the older woman shook her head sadly. "I'm afraid they're right, Pilar."

"He's done nothing wrong," she protested.

Andrew glared at Cored. "Tell me why you decided to have sex with a man you just met...a man almost ten years senior to you. He's *thirty*, Pilar. You've never looked at a man more than four years your senior before, and you've never even kissed another man. It's damned odd, you must admit."

"That was *my* decision to make," Pilar exploded. "Despite the Breeding Office, Maum and Dahd decided to let me act like any other noblewoman. I make love to whomever I want...when I want. I have that right."

"Obviously wherever you want, as well," Carter quipped, earning him a combined warning look from his entire family. "Sorry," he offered in a kit-toned voice.

"Make love?" Alex the younger asked, his cynicism not fully masked.

Pilar placed her fists on her hips. "You are the *last* person who should make judgments," she informed him. "Even if I decided to take after you, it would be no one's business but my own."

Cored swallowed a laugh, his throat aching in the effort.

Alex the younger had chosen to perform his duty of reproducing by studding genetically-superior children on lowborn women in contracts that wouldn't produce them naturally. It was all very civilized, with prospective matches being approved by the Breeding Office and contracts signed by the couple who would raise the child. It was amusing that what Alex the younger did was seen as noble, and what Cored did was a necessary evil.

Pilar wasn't done yet. "I have that right. Cored is of strong genetic stock. Even if I conceived—"

"What did he do?" Andrew growled. "Did he bring his genetic tests to bed with him? Oh. Wait. I forgot. He didn't have the courtesy to wait for a bed...or a woman healer for your first time."

"Of course not," she shouted, her face a vivid red.

Alex the elder motioned for his daughter's attention. "Then how can you know he's strong stock?" he inquired with a raising of his eyebrow that punctuated his line of thinking.

Pilar darkened to an alarming crimson, shooting Cored a pained look. She hadn't meant to tell them she needed healing...until she was healed, but she was healed now.

"Because he told you, and you trusted him?" Andrew accused.

"Do you think I'm that naïve?" she snapped.

"Then how?" Lyssa prodded.

Pilar groaned, her next glance at Cored pleading for some way out of the situation.

He sighed. "I healed her," he admitted. "She knows, because I possess the healing magic."

Pilar went wide-eyed, her expression fluctuating between amazement and dismay.

Cored shrugged. "Surely you meant to tell them *something*," he defended himself.

"If I wanted them to know I needed healing, why would I worry about getting healed first?"

"Ah. I see. Well, considering the fact that you told me you only worried about Andrew learning you needed healing, and were perfectly willing to entertain the thought of Alex healing you, if I could tell them apart. I've managed to figure that part out, now...just as an aside. So, you—"

"Well, Andrew knows now, doesn't he?" she pointed out in exasperation.

Cored grimaced, nodding. "I suppose he does."

"And just what were you healing?" Andrew asked.

No matter how Cored started that discussion, there was a chance of it turning ugly, so he left it to Pilar.

She rubbed the base of her skull beneath her blonde braid. "Uh... Well, there was a little matter with Loryol," she began.

Cored snorted at her understatement. "Little matter? The man left a bruise on you that needed healing."

She cleared her throat, shifting from foot to foot. "Yes, but you stopped—" Pilar glanced up at Andrew's tensing form and fell silent, dropping a step closer to Cored.

"What did Loryol do?" Andrew managed through clenched teeth.

Pilar sighed, rolling her neck as if to ease tension. "Tried to seduce me," she admitted.

"Seduction doesn't leave bruises," her abrasive older brother countered.

She grimaced.

Cored shook his head, abruptly weary. "No, it doesn't. But turning away a scheming—"

"What?" Carter asked, paling, no doubt at the thought of what Cored was implying.

Andrew shot his younger brother a scathing look. "And *that* is why we have a duty to protect Pilar," he snapped. "Loryol. Gods, you let her walk away with Loryol."

Carter swallowed hard and nodded, his color returning in a rush. "I didn't know," he whispered.

"Now you do." Andrew focused on Pilar again. "Did Loryol force you?"

She shook her head. "He just wouldn't let me leave the clearing."

"So you had sex with Cored out of...what...thanks?"

Alex the younger motioned for his twin's attention. "It's more likely that the healing affected her."

Cored furrowed his brow, working at that statement. "The healing?" What were they talking about? Healing just...healed. There were no other effects.

Andrew scowled at her. "You didn't think of that? You didn't consider it before you asked a strange man to heal you?"

Pilar raised her chin in challenge. "Your healing never felt like...that, and I would have made love to Cored anyway."

Lyssa groaned. "The effect of healing on the human genes is hard to ignore," she added.

Andrew shot Cored a furious look. "He never should have touched her in that state."

Cored raised his bound hands, completely lost and frustrated by it. "What *state*?" he demanded. "I have no idea what you're going on about."

"It's not common knowledge," Alex the elder noted. "Jole made sure it wouldn't be."

Alex the younger nodded his agreement. "He might not have known why Pilar was in a mating frenzy."

Lyssa touched her husband's arm, drawing his attention to her. "We usually heal our own. It's not the sort of thing we want the unscrupulous knowing."

Unscrupulous. That's me. Still... "*What* isn't common knowledge?" And why was it such a big secret?

Pilar met his gaze. "The human genetics affect how we experience the healing magic. It is—" She lowered her face, averting her eyes. "Well, it's rather arousing, to tell the truth."

Cored stared at her for a long moment then burst out laughing. "You were—"

She nodded miserably, and he laughed harder. Beneath it, his heart ached. He'd thought she trusted him...liked him, and all along, it had been a phantom of emotions brought on by his healing.

"I don't find this amusing," Andrew snapped at him.

Cored managed to stifle his outburst to a severe case of chuckling. "You're not the one in shackles. I think I've earned the right to be amused by how I ended up here."

"You're not in shackles because you healed Pilar. You're in shackles because you *fowked* her."

Pilar winced at whatever English word her brother had used. "How dare you," she fumed.

Andrew jerked his head in Cored's direction. "What do you think his aim was? He wanted to force you to a Trial Moon."

She shook her head, denying it.

"Ask him. Let's see if he can lie to you about it, because...trust me, he *will* be lying if he claims he didn't intend it."

Pilar turned to Cored, her eyes begging for affirmation. She needed to believe he was innocent; Cored didn't even need his extra senses to tell him that.

His heart ached. Cored didn't want lies between them, which was ironic, considering the fact that he'd set out to lie, if needs be. He didn't want to hurt her either, and the truth was going to hurt.

"You were going to demand a Trial Moon," Andrew insisted. "Weren't you?"

Cored nodded. She deserved the truth. "I was. I wanted that chance."

"You set into sex with that in mind?" he pressed.

"Of course, I considered it," Cored barked, hating Andrew nearly as much as he hated himself. "Any sane man would have considered it, but that wasn't..."

Pilar's eyes filled with tears.

"It's not how it sounds," Cored whispered. "Please believe me. It's not all I want."

"No," Andrew accused. "You want your title back. A disavowed lord only has so many ways to ascend again. Pilar was your pass back into polite society."

Cored grimaced. "Before I met you—"

Pilar punched him hard across the jaw, rocking his head back. Cored didn't need his senses to interpret that move any more than he had her need to believe him innocent. Pilar was hurt; she was humiliated. She hated him.

"I'm sorry," he whispered. "It's really not what it seems."

Andrew moved to pull Pilar to his chest, but she sidestepped him neatly, brushing past Cored then away from both of them.

Pilar wiped the tears from her cheeks. "Men," she cursed. "I don't want anything to do with the lot of you." She looked at her father, Alex the younger, and Carter, gathered around the desk. "Not the three of you." She met Cored's gaze. "Not—" Pilar swallowed down a sob. "Not you." She turned on Andrew, adding that same pointing finger for emphasis. "And especially not you."

She marched out the door, her head high and shoulders back, slamming it behind her.

Cored closed his eyes, sick more from the harm he'd done Pilar than the fact that he'd never have a chance to claim a re-bred bride now. Cullin had won, and Cored no longer cared that he had.

"Release him," Alex the elder ordered. "Get him off this estate. If you come near my daughter or land again, I will have your head."

Cored nodded, grumbling his understanding. What was left to come back for?

CHAPTER THREE

Jad 13, Ri 25-3016

"Coming," Cored slurred, weaving toward the door with the decanter of iri brandy clutched in his hand. He dragged the door open, stilling at the sight of Pilar on his stoop.

He released the door and rubbed a hand over his face, certain that he was hallucinating. What possible reason could Pilar have for coming here? What could make her look so haunted?

"May I enter?" she asked formally.

Cored nodded, moving back to let her pass.

Pilar cast her gaze about, seemingly interested in how a disavowed lord lived. "Very nice," she offered.

"A woman comes in to clean three times a week. I'm pretty hopeless without her." That wasn't strictly true. He'd survived without it before he'd resigned himself to peddling his genetic code to improve his lot in life. He bit back a wince at the truth that it was hardly an improvement in his situation, but rather a trade of one unpleasant task for another.

"It's very...comfortable." She ambled further into the library, looking at the first shelf of books though he doubted she was interested in his tastes in reading.

"Why are you here, Pilar?"

She met his gaze, her expression unreadable. "You hurt me."

27

He grimaced. "I know. I tried to explain."

"I don't want explanations."

"What *do* you want?" It was likely she wanted to tell him what a worthless geela he was. If she did, he'd let her. It wouldn't be anything he hadn't thought of himself in the last few days.

She turned her attention to the waning fire. "I want what we started. I want you to finish—"

"You want me to have sex with you?" he asked, certain that this was a hallucination.

Pilar looked back, a wounded look marring her beauty, making her appear worn. The calm indifference that took its place didn't improve matters. "Yes. I do."

"Why?"

She seemed uncertain for a moment. Then the practiced calm returned. "You owe me that much consideration," she decided.

Cored fumbled the brandy onto the table beside her, ignoring it as it toppled, spilled its contents over the surface, and streamed onto the rug. He cupped her face, opening himself to her emotions.

She did feel he owed her this. There was a self-serving, mercenary bent to her emotions. Pilar's trusting nature was gone. In its place was fear, anger, mistrust...but there was a glimmer of something warm, buried beneath the rest. What it was, he couldn't say...perhaps hope, but of what?

He pressed his lips to hers, and she gasped in response.

"Yes. I'll give you what you came here for." *Why not? I've given other women the same. Maybe I can pretend she trusts me, that she loves me.*

He'd never wanted to pretend the nobles he'd sold himself to cared for him, but he wanted that with Pilar.

No, I want it to be real, but I can't have that wish.

She nodded, rising up as she had the first time she kissed him, her hands fisting in his robe, her mouth frantic against his.

"No. Slowly. Enjoy what I'm going to do to you."

Cored drew her dress over her head and tossed it to the floor. Pilar kicked her short boots away while he untied his robe and flung it toward her dress.

Pilar panned her gaze down his body, biting her lip at the sight of the erect length straining toward her. She eased forward, trapping his cock between her thighs.

He groaned, rocking his hips to drive the shaft through her waiting fluids. Pilar arched her back, planting her head against the edge of the bookcase, positioning herself so that the head of his cock pressed against her swollen slit at every pass.

Cored thrust up into her, lifting her body off the floor on the plane of his hips, drinking in Pilar's moan of pleasure. He grasped her hips in his hands, steadying her for more.

"Yes," she breathed.

His echoed agreement came out a rasping half-breath. He started moving inside her in slow, deep thrusts, thankful that the iri brandy would stave off his release. What he planned to do to Pilar would take time.

She stroked her hands down his chest, her eyes half-closed in pleasure and her breathing erratic. She was beautiful, captivating. He couldn't have looked away from her if he wanted to.

Cored watched her, spellbound, drinking in every emotion that flitted through her fevered mind and breast. She wanted this, craved it, needed to experience what he had to offer. Cored had been wrong. It wasn't a mercenary streak in Pilar but rather a need so deep that she was riding the edges of madness because of it.

"Take it," he breathed.

Her climax was close. He could feel it drawing at her and closed his inner self to it. If he didn't, Cored would follow her over. Pilar wanted completion. Cored wouldn't give her that until they'd enjoyed a lot more than this rushed encounter. He groaned, steeling himself as her sheath rippled around him.

Pilar's fingernails bit into his shoulders. She latched her legs around his hips and pulled him to the hilt. "Now," she begged. "Please, Cored. Now."

"Not yet."

She opened her eyes, suspicion staring out at him. It had a crippling effect on him.

"Why?" she demanded.

"Because that's not what you really want." *It's not what I want, either.*

"It is," she insisted. "That's why I'm here."

Cored shook his head. A schaen could give Pilar simple completion. A schaen could release an egg of her. Pilar was here for something more.

"I don't know what," she started to rage at him.

He drew her mouth to his. Pilar came at him in unrestrained need. Cored guided the kiss to a slow exploration. Her hands fisted in his hair, and Cored opened himself to her emotions again.

Her arousal was rising steadily, but the rest of her emotions were rioting. She did want this. Cored could only assume her confusion stemmed from the fact that she hadn't expected him to slow for her. She'd expected him to be fast and rough, to take her without regard.

Cored pressed her to his body, making his way unsteadily down the corridor. Pilar would know precisely what she could expect from him soon.

He hit something solid, reeling around it on the pivot point of his hip, elbowing a pair of oculars off of what he now recognized as the small table in the corridor. The glass shattered and the table overturned, clunking hard on the door frame, but he disregarded it as a minor annoyance and kept moving.

Pilar broke away from the kiss, looking around them in surprise. "What are you doing?"

"Having the courtesy to stimulate your first egg in a bed," he answered calmly, his heart pounding in anticipation.

"Your bed," she breathed.

"Yes. Mine." A fierce possessiveness he had no right to feel welled up in him. When she left him, this was all Cored would have left—the memories of having her now...of having her first.

Pilar looked up at him from his silin sheets, one of the few luxuries his stipend bought him. Cored was abruptly thankful for his healing magic. His abilities granted him aid he wouldn't be due otherwise. Pilar deserved silin sheets. It was one of the few things she deserved that he could give her.

"Now?" she asked, dragging him back to the more immediate pleasures she had in mind.

Cored shook his head, easing her thighs apart and backing out of her fisting heat. He didn't give her time to protest the move, taking a nipple in his mouth and savoring the pink treat. She tasted of Gelgrin and musk.

She grasped at his hair again, sinking into his care. Cored loved at each of her breasts in turn: suckling, licking at them, pulling at them gently with his teeth. Then he moved down her body, bathing the musk from her skin.

He paused at her womb, laying a kiss over it reverently. Would he give her a child? Cored shivered, hoping he would. He sobered. It would be Pilar's child, if he did, as the noblewomen he impregnated had their children.

There would be no Trial Moon, and with the new re-bred laws, the child would still be hers if he asked for one. All Cored would have would be his stipend. He didn't want money. He didn't want position...not anymore. If Cored couldn't have Pilar, he didn't want anything from her...past what they were enjoying at the moment.

Cored wondered, fleetingly, if Alex the younger would be appalled to learn that Cored had made a decent living at Alex's chosen duty of impregnating women of strong genetic stock, spreading the strongest genes as far as he could and as far as a noblewoman's gold went.

Unlike Alex, Cored was paid well for his work. Not that the oldest Braeden son needed money like Cored did. Unlike Alex, Cored spent as much time with a woman as she wanted and paid for. To date, only three of his clients had left Cored still childless.

He shook off that thought and moved on. Pilar wasn't a mercenary noblewoman paying the stud for his time. She wanted him, at least for this.

Pilar cried out in surprise as Cored stroked his tongue along her seam. She gasped out a 'no,' though her emotions called her a liar.

Cored swirled his tongue around her hood, smiling at her groan. "This is what you came here for," he assured her.

"No," she denied. "Just completion."

"The sweeter the journey, the sweeter the release."

She hesitated. "Is it?"

"Oh, yes." Cored stroked the tip of his tongue through her nether lips, growing dizzy on her musk.

Pilar rolled her head back and forth on the pillow, tipping her hips up for his attentions. She was responsive, more responsive than any noblewoman he'd had. There would be no need of Dolgen with her. Cored felt certain he could grow hard, time and again, just from the sight of her, the taste of her, her haunting scent and sounds.

He pushed her knees out, bracing them apart as he thrust his tongue in and found her pleasure spot. Pilar moved abruptly, nearly escaping his embrace.

"Cored," she pleaded. "I can't—" Pilar broke off on a scream of delight, her body contracting around him and granting him the nectar she released.

He rose up over her, turning to his back beside her, his body aching to finish it. Cored fought back the urge to give in. Once he stimulated her band, Pilar would have no reason to stay.

Her deep blue eyes met his, dilated in her need for completion. "Now?" she asked.

Cored shook his head slowly. Gods, but this was maddening. He'd come to climax after climax personally, but he'd never realized how frustrating it would be to deny himself while performing the same feat for another.

Pilar rose up over him, straddling his hips and impaling herself on his length. "Yes," she insisted.

He waited too long to shut her emotions out. Pilar's need was too strong, her arousal too fierce.

She pushed herself up on her knees and drove down onto him again, forcing him to the gates of her womb. Pilar started to rise again, but Cored locked her body to his, shaking his head in a mute wish that he could hold off the climax already rushing through him. His seed seemed to jet into her with the force of an explosion.

"Yes," she breathed. "Oh, yes. Please don't stop."

Cored couldn't have stopped if he tried. He managed a strangled cry as his cock swelled, squeezed tight by her stim band. Pilar's scream overpowered his.

"So hot," she murmured, pressing a hand to her womb. She laid over him, seeking his mouth, not frantic now but slow and solemn, as if the act of completion eased some great tension she'd harbored.

Cored's heart ached. Pilar had what she'd come for. She would leave him now. He sent up hopeless prayers that he wouldn't lessen, that he could hold this moment forever...or at least for more than the next few minutes. Cored swallowed down a sob as he released her band. It was over.

She laid her head to his shoulder, shivering. Pilar traced the lines of his chest, muttering something unintelligible. Her hand relaxed. Her cheek settled against his skin, nuzzling into him as a kittle-kit would in search of mother's milk.

He moved cautiously, unable to trust his luck. Cored stroked the flat of his hand up her spine, examining the even rise and fall that indicated deep sleep. He tangled his fingers in her hair, combing through the dark gold waves.

"Asleep," he whispered, terrified of waking her. This was more than he'd dared hope for. While she slept, Cored could pretend Pilar was his. When she woke, she would leave him as every other woman had.

CHAPTER FOUR

"*Damn it*," Andrew cursed in English. Pilar's transport was in front of Cored's cottage, just as he'd feared.

"Don't jump to conclusions," Alex chided him.

"You think she hasn't had sex with that *bastard* by now?" he snapped.

"Probably, but if she did, she chose to. Pilar came here willingly. Cored didn't kidnap her."

"She's played right into his hands," Andrew complained.

"Willingly! Pilar is an adult. She has to be allowed to make her own choices."

Andrew ground his teeth in frustration. Of course, his twin wouldn't appreciate the gravity of this situation. After all, the man played stud twice a month. He was the ultimate bachelor. "Adult or not, you know what Dad said."

Alex sighed. "Cored didn't pursue her. Dad can call Jole in, and the decision will be for Cored."

"Then Jole will make the decision," he growled.

He nodded, seemingly exasperated with Andrew. "We'll take him in, but hands off. If you hit him, he'll have the right to press charges."

Andrew glared at the door to his adversary's home. "As long as he hasn't mistreated Pilar, Cored will make it to trial in one piece."

The door was locked. Alex raised a hand to knock, but Andrew grasped his wrist, stilling him. He unsheathed his dagger.

Alex shook his head. "You have no right to—"

"Until proven innocent," Andrew growled. "Pilar is a re-bred."

He snapped the lock with a muted crunch of metal against metal, then pushed the door wide. The smell of iri brandy assaulted him first. Andrew curled his nose in distaste and strode inside. Pilar's dress and Cored's robe lay crumpled on the library floor, soaked with the brandy that had spilled from the table above. Andrew's hand tightened on the hilt of his dagger reflexively.

"Put it away," Alex ordered quietly, as if reading his thoughts.

He sheathed his dagger with a snort of disgust, then turned down the corridor. Andrew stared at the upset table and shattered oculars for a moment, unsure whether the idea of Cored on a rampage or in the midst of sexual abandon with Pilar bothered him more. He moved on, stilling again in the bedroom doorway.

Pilar was there, asleep in Cored's arms, her gold hair tossed over his chest, hiding her face. A silin sheet covered them from the waist down, but Andrew could clearly see Cored's leg tucked between her thighs.

"Get up," he barked, his anger rising fast at the possessive way the criminal held her.

Pilar startled, sitting up abruptly and looking at him with wide eyes.

Beside her, Cored groaned, running a hand over his face. He squinted at Pilar, then at Andrew and Alex. "What in Len's Unholy Underworld do you want?" he grumbled.

"You were warned to stay away from Pilar."

She blushed deeply, crossing her arms over her breasts. "I came here," she reminded them. "You have no right—"

"I have every right. He should have turned you away."

"Why?" she argued stubbornly.

Alex grasped Andrew's shoulder, then spoke calmly. "Get up, Pilar. You too, Cored."

Cored rubbed at his temples, no doubt suffering an iri brandy headache. "Let me get this in perspective. You broke into my home, where your sister is a guest, to arrest me?"

Pilar nodded. "That would seem to be the case."

"Pilar..." Alex reasoned.

"I am an adult, and I am tired of you two treating me like a child. Go home. I'll be there when I'm good and ready." She scowled at Andrew. "And you will pay for whatever you broke to get in."

Andrew dragged off his tunic and threw it at Pilar. "Put this on—now!" He caught it as she threw it back at him.

"Put it on yourself."

He stormed to her, grasped Pilar by her upper arms, and hauled her struggling form over his shoulder. He looked up in surprise as Cored launched off the bed at him, but Alex was there first, his dagger pressed to the man's throat in warning. For a moment, they stared at each other.

"Don't," Alex growled. "My father has no legal recourse. I know that, and you know that, but we have to take you with us to settle it. Please, stand down."

"Put her down," Cored bargained. "I'll get dressed and come quietly if you let her go."

Pilar stopped squirming. "They have no right to do this," she argued.

Cored sighed. "It know it, but that rarely stops the nobility. No offense to you, of course."

"None taken. I'd be glad to be rid of the lot of them." Pilar laid a sloppy punch on Andrew's shoulder. "Let me down."

"You'll put on the tunic?" Andrew asked pointedly. "You'll—"

"Never. I'd rather die than wear your tunic."

Cored motioned Alex away and turned toward the door. "I'll get your dress."

"Don't bother," Andrew informed him. "It's ruined...soaked in brandy."

"I don't care," Pilar snapped. "I'll go nude before I wear your tunic."

Cored's jaw tightened, and he shot a glance at Alex, then Andrew. "Will you wear one of mine?" he asked.

"No," Andrew answered for her. "She won't."

Pilar tried to kick her way down again, growling when Andrew immobilized her legs. "Oh, let me down," she complained. Under her breath, she muttered something that sounded of a promise to bite his ass, if he didn't comply.

"You'll wear the tunic? You'll walk out of here calmly?"

"Yes and yes. Now put me down."

Andrew set her on her feet and extended his hand with the tunic still clutched in his fist.

Pilar turned on her heel and strode to Cored, smiling. "Where would one find a tunic?" she inquired sweetly.

Alex grasped Andrew by the arm. "Give up while she isn't fighting," he advised.

"She is not wearing his tunic," Andrew insisted. "Not when we're taking him to judgment."

Pilar turned to them, paling. She stepped back, nestling her back to Cored's chest and seeking his hand with hers. "There is no judgment. You don't have a choice."

"What do you mean?" Andrew demanded.

"I came to Cored and offered myself. What do you think I mean?"

"Pilar," Cored cautioned her. "Andrew is the wrong person to—"

"We have to inform someone," she reasoned. "My older brothers are close enough. They act like overprotective parents." Pilar met Andrew's gaze. "Cored demanded a Trial Moon. I'm not filing a grievance. By law, you can't intervene."

Alex placed himself between them, holding Andrew back when he surged toward Cored to throttle him. "She's right. You can't interfere. He has thirty-seven days to win his contract."

Andrew glared at Cored. "And his title," he growled.

Cored didn't reply to the accusation. The former lord wrapped an arm around Pilar's waist and leaned to whisper in her ear, most probably thanks for saving his worthless skin. And if Pilar didn't fight the Trial Moon, his skin was decidedly safe.

Alex leaned close enough to whisper in Andrew's ear. "Maybe her heir will be enough for her. Jole's new laws award the child to the re-bred, male or female. Pilar knows that."

Something told Andrew it wasn't going to be that simple.

* * * *

"Are you insane?" Cored whispered, fighting back the attack of nerves warring with relief. Laws or no laws, Pilar's father might have made a case that would have seen Cored dead. Pilar's lie ensured that he couldn't be tried.

Still, he hadn't asked for this. Why, no matter what path he sought to take with Pilar, did he end up with an opposite result? "I didn't ask for a Trial Moon. I had no intention of forcing you to—"

Pilar turned in his arms, hiding the hurt in her eyes. Why was it that trying to put her at ease hurt her? Why could he never make the right choice with her?

Her voice was deceptively calm. "One month of your time and you're free." She pressed closer to him, and Andrew tensed behind her. "It's worth one month, isn't it?"

Cored avoided her emotions, sure of what he'd find. This was a contract of sorts. Pilar would have her heir in exchange for his freedom, and Cored would be rewarded handsomely for his services as stud, better than he ever had been before.

He nodded. "As you wish." It had always come to this, to what people could use him for.

"Good. Then we should dress."

Cored released her and pulled out one of his formal tunics. The long silver silin tunic reached nearly to Pilar's knees. He cuffed the sleeves for her, then tied the neckline to just above her breasts. Cored stared down at her for a moment, stunned. She looked far too good in his tunic...better than his sanity would withstand, possibly.

Pilar smoothed the silin over her thighs and blushed, scooping a lock of her pale hair behind her ear.

"Your clothing, Cored," Andrew reminded him.

He nodded, pulling on a matching tunic to the one Pilar wore, then his best black trousers and boots. He paused with his hand on his belt. "I suppose my dagger would be unwelcome," he noted.

"It would," Alex answered.

"Very well." Cored turned and offered Pilar his arm.

Andrew scowled as she took her place at his Cored's side, but her brother wisely remained silent and waved them out of the cottage.

* * * *

Pilar sighed, fighting the urge to smooth the tunic down her thighs again.

Why did I think this was a good plan? Her father didn't have any right to ask for a judgment on Cored, but Cored didn't trust that the nobility abided by the laws that should have protected him. Pilar couldn't let them punish Cored for her mad urges.

That's all it had been. She'd spent days, curled in her bed, dozing fitfully, dreaming of their time in the garden, waking aching as she had when Alex had pulled Cored out of her. It had been driving her mad. Pilar had considered consulting her woman healer about it, but she was afraid Nolga would tell her she was crazy.

So I did something crazy to prove it? What was wrong with her?

"You're certain about this?" her father asked, shooting Cored a look that promised retribution.

"I'm sure," she replied. "I'm not fighting the Trial Moon."

He nodded grimly. "Will you be staying here?"

"No."

"Yes," Cored stated at the same time.

Pilar shot him a look of disbelief. "Here? With my brothers watching our every move? Listening at doors? Not acceptable." She'd never pull this off if Andrew was allowed to barge in at any time.

"My home lacks the comforts you're accustomed to."

"It has privacy." She scowled at Andrew. "Or...it will, once you have the lock you destroyed replaced."

"I cook for myself," Cored warned her.

"Then you can teach me," she reasoned in reply.

"I'm not that good."

Pilar smirked at him, tempted to make the most of the set-up he'd dealt her.

Cored darkened, shooting Andrew a pained look. "All right," he decided. "My home it is."

"I knew you'd see it my way." Pilar swallowed down a sigh of relief. Without Andrew over her shoulder, this plan would work. Just one month with him, and Cored was a free man.

"I trust you'll dress now?" Andrew suggested.

Pilar smiled sweetly and batted her eyes at him, sighing for effect when Andrew's eyes narrowed. "I think not. I rather enjoy wearing Cored's tunic. It's rather...*Bohemian*, don't you think?"

Alex shook his head, his jaw tightening. "When are you going to learn that she'll do the opposite of whatever you order her to do?"

Pilar chuckled. "Alexander Joseph Braeden, I do believe you are the second most intelligent of my brothers."

"Second?" he asked, his eyes narrowed in suspicion.

"Yes. Carter is smart enough to keep quiet and stay out of my way." Pilar strode out of her father's office with Cored in her wake.

* * * *

Pilar seemed to get more nervous and less animated as they drew closer to Cored's home. He ground his teeth at the reaction, wondering what he could do to put her at ease.

"Why did you really want to stay at my home?" he asked, maneuvering her personal transport around a curve.

Pilar shrugged. "Privacy. In case you haven't noticed, I don't get much of it."

"You don't want to flaunt this in front of your brothers?" he asked pointedly. She'd made a good show of doing that thus far.

"No. Would you?"

Cored grimaced. He would. Cored would love to have his family see him with Pilar on his arm.

She looked up at him curiously. "You would."

"I'm not perfect, Pilar. I have a taste for vengeance, but I didn't plan this Trial Moon...and I won't use it to find my vengeance." It was a vow he'd never envisioned making, but it felt right.

Pilar hesitated, staring out the window, her throat bobbing. "Thank you." She didn't look at him when she said it.

The rest of the way passed in silence. Cored lifted her bag from the rear seat of her transport before Pilar could and waved her toward the cottage. She pushed the door wide and entered, scowling at the still-broken lock.

Cored kicked the door shut and brushed past her into the bedroom. He set the bag on the bed and opened the cabinet, moving his clothing aside for her.

"That's not necessary," Pilar noted.

"What isn't?" he replied.

"Making room for me. I won't be here long." There was a note of cynicism in her voice.

"It's yours as long as you are," he growled, bristling at the reminder that she was only here to secure her heir. "You can't live out of a bag the whole month. What if your brothers visit and see it?"

Pilar sighed. "You're right, I suppose."

Cored moved away, giving her the space to store her clothes. He swallowed as she leaned over her bag, his tunic riding high on her thighs. His cock was abruptly hard and aching for her, despite his place as well-paid stud.

As if in a trance, he stepped behind her, running his fingertips up her hips, envisioning her sounds as he slid inside.

"What..." she gasped. "What are you doing?"

"Keeping my part of our bargain." He eased his hands under the tunic, pulling Pilar into the cradle of his hips.

"Bargain?" she asked, seemingly stunned.

"Your heir for my freedom."

Cored reached for the ties over her breasts. Pilar elbowed him in the ribs, spinning out of his arms and away from his body with wide eyes and a shaking head. He pressed a hand to the rising bruise, grimacing at her sense of placement.

"You think—" She took a violent lungful of air. "Let me set your mind at ease, Cored. I don't push myself at any man."

He snorted in disbelief, motioning to his painfully-tight trousers. "Do I look like I'm being forced?" he demanded.

"Did I ask for an heir?" She forged on without waiting for an answer. "I asked for a Trial Moon to save your skin, not to secure a fertile schaen to play with."

Pilar dragged off his tunic and threw it at him, much as she had with Andrew. That move gave Cored a brief but torturous glimpse of her body. In the next moment, she was covering it with one of her robes and belting it shut.

"I meant what I said," she huffed. "In a month, you are free from harm and free of me. Until then—"

"You don't want sex from me?" he asked, confused. Why would she do this if not with a thought of some payment?

Her face darkened, and her eyes flashed a vivid shade of blue. Pilar planted her fists on her hips. "Sex? I assure you that *sex* is the last thing I want from you." She stormed toward the doorway, stiff in fury.

"Where are you going now?" he shouted after her, as stung by her dismissal as he'd been when he believed she wanted him for an heir.

"To bed."

"There's only one bed," he reminded her.

"Don't be ridiculous. I've intruded on your home. I will be quite comfortable on your lounging couch."

He plodded after her, sighing. "You don't have to be afraid to share a bed with me," he informed her. "I don't touch unwilling women."

"Really?" she challenged.

"You didn't seem unwilling to me."

"When I struck you?" she snapped, turning to face him in the corridor.

"No. A moment earlier, when your breasts were tight as pins and your scent was driving me mad."

Her jaw notched down in anger. "You needn't worry about it any longer. For the remainder of the month, it would be best if we simply kept our distance."

"You really did this for no better reason than saving my neck?"

"You thought I wanted to pay you for the honor of having your child?" she countered hotly.

"Why not?" he grumbled. *Other noblewomen have.* "What do you plan to do if we've already produced a child?"

Pilar hesitated, shifting from foot to foot. "I'll dissolve and make you a very rich man for an afternoon of work." She swallowed some powerful emotion and painted that Len-be-damned cold look on her lovely face. "I'm sure that would break your heart," she accused.

A knock echoed through the cottage.

"Come in," Pilar shouted.

Cored turned around her, shielding her with his body. "Are you crazy?" he whispered fiercely. "This isn't your manor, Pilar. You're not dressed appropriately for guests."

She glanced around his shoulder. Her eyes narrowed, and she rose to him, meeting his lips fervently, her hands fisting in his tunic and dragging him to her.

Cored ceased to question Pilar's bouncing libido, too aroused to care what mad thought had pushed her toward him this time. If she was willing, Pilar would learn what a woman he desired could expect from him.

His hands closed on her hips, and he crushed her to his erection, his final warning for what he intended. Pilar tipped her hips to him, seeking his cock, her hands skating over his neck to pull his lips to hers.

"Mag alive! Don't you have more control than that?"

Cored pulled away at the snide voice from the doorway, his hands tightening on her hips in realization. She'd used him...again.

Pilar smiled, a harsh twisting of her lips. "No, Andrew. I don't have more self-control than this."

Oh, but she will learn, he decided. Pilar was done using Cored in her games.

CHAPTER FIVE

Pilar sighed at the vision of Cored in her mind. His hands stroked at her skin, his teeth nipping at the column of her throat. She groaned his name, her body heating for more.

His chuckle cut through the last of the sleep clouding her mind. "That's right," he crooned.

She braced a hand against his bare chest, struggling to focus her sleep-starved eyes. "What are you doing?" she demanded.

"Convincing you," he breathed, ducking his head around her arm to lay a kiss on the upper swell of her breast.

"Convincing me to what?" Pilar wriggled away from him on the couch.

"There is the little matter of our Trial Moon," Cored replied patiently, drawing her back to his body, proving himself the stronger of the two.

Pilar shivered as his cock pressed to her mound through dual layers of silin. She remembered all too well what that cock felt like thrusting inside her. "We have no Trial Moon," she snapped, trying to shut her thighs a moment too late to stop him from sliding a leg between them to nestle to her already-aroused core. "It was a lie."

"Not anymore," he warned.

"I don't—"

"The sun hasn't risen on a new day yet, Pilar. I have until sunrise to demand the Trial Moon you started by coming to my bed, and I'm asking."

"You can't," she wailed.

"I can. Legally, I have the right, and you have no right to stop me."

"I'll—" Pilar groaned, most likely in the realization that she had no legal recourse. "I've already forfeit my rights to challenge it," she noted miserably.

"Exactly."

"You promised not to use this against me," she pleaded.

"When I thought we had a mutual agreement. You've used me, Pilar. Over and over again, you have. You used me to sate yourself, and every time your brother comes near you, you use me to infuriate him." He traced one nipple with the pad of his thumb. "By law, I have the right to convince you." His voice grew rough in arousal.

Pilar shook her head in denial. She'd settled for sex with Cored once. She had no intentions of making that mistake again. "I won't be convinced," she warned him.

"Won't you?" It was a challenge.

"No. I won't." But her stomach was already fluttering in excitement that Cored intended to try. Meaningless sex or not, he was a talented male. The idea of sex with Cored was more enticing than she'd ever found the idea of making love with another man. If only she could recapture the moment when she'd believed she was making love with *him.*

Cored stroked her nipple again, and Pilar flicked his hand away, feigning indifference. He shot her a look of surprise, then smiled. His fingers parted her robe beneath the tie, and she moved away, clamping her thighs shut when she cleared his knee.

"Go to your bed, Cored," she growled at him.

"I think I'll stay here." He eased his hands away, looking entirely too pleased with him self.

And wait for me to sleep again. Convincing her would be easier if she was asleep and unable to stifle her responses. He could enflame her and take advantage of her mating frenzy.

Pilar didn't question that this wasn't acceptance of her refusal. He would try again. "Then I will use the bed," she decided, turning away from him and moving to rise.

Cored's arms wrapped around her, and his lips pressed to the back of her neck. Pilar started to push his hands away in frustration.

She stiffened as the shaft of ice pierced her and raced over her nerves like wildfire. *Oh, no. The healing magic. That will—* Pilar barely registered Cored's intent when the heat coursed over the chilled route and pleasure in its wake.

"Please," she begged. He couldn't do this. If he did, she'd be in a frenzy in moments. It was precisely the reason they didn't tell the general public what the healing magic did to re-breds.

"As you wish." The next spike of cold started at the pulse point in her throat.

Pilar groaned, turning toward him in the circle of his loosening arms. She shook her head, but her plea for an end to this game came to a halt as the heat and pleasure assaulted her. Her eyes slid shut, and she arched toward Cored, energized, her entire body alive to sensation.

Cored's lips skated over hers, bringing that flash of ice. Pilar trembled, crying out as his healing undid her resolve.

"Convinced?" he teased, opening the tie on her robe with nimble fingers.

She shook her head, her breathing ragged.

His fingertips moved up her inner thighs, as if determined to prove her a liar in the slight parting he'd accomplished, in the slick of her fluids gathering in preparation for him.

She jumped in surprise as he stroked her inner thigh, finding erogenous zones she'd only been lectured on. Pilar resigned herself to failure.

"Give yourself to me," he requested.

Pilar rocked up against his hand, spreading her legs for his body. Cored's fingers didn't breach her body. He spread her folds open, shifting his body to fit the engorged head of his cock inside her.

She met his eyes, desperate for his loving. That's what she really wanted, what she'd always wanted—his love, but that was something Cored wouldn't give her.

* * * *

Cored prepared to teach Pilar her lesson. She wanted him. All he had to do was leave her wanting. He had to show her how he could use her as she'd used him, exciting him and not paying due.

Pilar looked up at him, tears pooled in her eyes. He stilled, opening his senses to her in confusion.

The need for him was stronger than he'd ever felt it, but there was more. There was a sense of desperation in Pilar, akin to a certainty that she wasn't going to have what she wanted most in life. Cored wished he had the ability to read coherent thoughts from her instead of these shattered sensations.

He stroked her face. "Tell me what you want," he whispered. "If you could have anything in the world, what would it be?"

Amazement lit in her, mixed with hope. She buried it ruthlessly, shaking her head and dislodging one fat tear onto her cheek. "Nothing," she lied. "There is nothing I want."

Cored scowled. She would never trust him. "Everyone wishes for something," he reasoned.

"Not something they can have. What is the good in wishing for something you cannot have?"

"One should always have hope."

"Have you?" she accused.

Cored shook his head, his face burning. "No. I haven't."

Pilar hiccupped on what was probably a sob. "I thought not."

He stroked the column of her throat. "Do you want this? If you really don't—"

Disbelief and panic warred in her, cracking her renewed calm exterior. Cored started to push away from her, aching in body and soul, as he always was when she refused him.

Pilar grasped at his arms, shaking her head frantically. "Don't leave," she begged. "Please, Cored."

"You want me?" he asked cautiously. He'd never met a woman who confused him as much as Pilar did.

"More than anything."

No. Not anything. There's something you want more. Or someone. He pushed that thought away.

Cored eased inside her, reveling in every hot, silin finger-width of her encasing him. Pilar shivered, tracing the muscles of his arms with a stunned look.

"Hold me," he instructed her, at the edges of control already.

Her legs wrapped tight around his waist, tilting her hips and opening her channel fully to him. She played her fingers in the curls at the base of his neck. "Now?" she asked.

"Now." His thrusts were deep, lodging hard to her womb with every roll of his hips.

Pilar groaned in delight, learning to meet him, guided in part by the hand cupped under her buttocks and in part by the Keen sex drive. Her fingers sought out the bundle of nerves at the base of his skull.

Cored gasped in surprise as she massaged the spot. He knew she'd been trained in sexual practices; all re-breds were. He hadn't expected Pilar to use that knowledge to give him pleasure. No noblewoman ever had.

He closed his eyes, drinking in the pulses of pleasure that radiated from her fingertips, through his body, and up the length of his cock. His sac tightened in the approaching climax, and his breathing degraded into gasping and half-formed prayers to Fion.

No, his mind protested. She had to come for him first. Cored buried his face in her throat, seeking out the source of her musk. He concentrated a burst of healing over the spot, knowing the response would radiate through her as her massage had through him.

Pilar dragged his mouth up to hers, her body contracting around his length, her tongue urgent against his. Cored lodged himself deep inside her, sweeping into her mouth as his cock emptied his body in a pleasant rush. He locked into her band, pulling his face back on a sigh.

The desperation from Pilar cut through his lingering release, and Cored looked down at her curiously. What was it she wanted? What was missing in her life?

Pilar looked away, reining in her needs, closing off her emotions as she did so often.

His cock lessened. Cored didn't leave her body immediately. "Do you want me to leave?" he asked.

Her eyes widened. "No. Of course... No."

"At least come to bed with me." It would be much more comfortable than the lounging couch.

She nodded, blushing crimson. "But..."

"Yes?" He'd agree to almost anything right now, and that thought shook him.

"I want your word that you won't try this again."

"What?" What in Len's name was her game this time?

Pilar hesitated. "I want your word that you won't..."

"That I won't try to convince you again?"

"Yes."

"That's what you want?" He knew it wasn't. *So...why is she asking for it?*

For a moment, she didn't answer. "Yes. It is."

Cored found it hard to form words. "Then you have my vow. Unless you approach me. If you tempt me, to annoy your brothers or not, I *will* finish what you start," he warned.

"A-agreed."

His heart sank at that one word. "Agreed."

CHAPTER SIX

Jad 21, Ri 25-3016

Pilar pulled another tin from the cabinet, opening it and inhaling deeply. "Mmmm. Tea," she sighed. It was a flavor she wasn't accustomed to, but the base scent seemed to be redroot.

She opened the oven, scowling at the roasting kit. There was no doubt her attempt would be lacking in comparison to her cooks', probably lacking in comparison to what Cored could prepare for himself, but Pilar had never attempted to cook a meal before. She'd gone through his stores of spices, container by container, using whatever smelled good in combination on the meat.

The marketplace near his home had been disconcerting, but she'd bought tubers to roast with the kit and fruits for dessert. Now there was little left to do but let the meal cook and wait for Cored to come home.

A smile settled on her face. Perhaps a cup of tea and a hot bath were in order.

She mixed the tea by guess, noting that a heaping spoon was a bit too strong. Perhaps she'd make the next cup with a level spoon.

Pilar filled the tub, adding an iri oil she'd found in the bath cabinet. By the time she sank in, half of the cup was gone.

The water relaxed her muscles, and the heat nearly drew her into sleep. She drank down the rest of the cup then started to bathe, her mind fixed on her plans for dinner.

Visions of Cored's enjoyment of her cooking surrendered to visions of him showing his appreciation for her efforts in the form of breaking his vow. Her body reacted fiercely to the image. The moving water tantalized her, making the ache for him more acute.

Pilar stroked her fingers over her hood, gasping at the pleasure it brought her. What she wouldn't give to feel Cored's mouth again.

It wasn't a smart wish. Her fascination with Cored made no sense. Though she didn't understand what drove Cored, it wasn't the same thing that drove her.

He confused her on many levels. He wanted a contract to ascend to the nobility again and perhaps to rebuild his fortune, but he'd agreed not to approach her sexually. And he'd kept his word, though the Trial Moon gave him the right to pursue her. She'd asked him for a rough fuck, offered herself for base sex, and he'd shown her tenderness. He'd convinced her to take him, then offered to stop.

Then there was his assumption that she'd wanted to bargain for an heir. He'd seemed genuinely confused that Pilar didn't want anything of the sort from him. What caused his certainty? Had he been sorely used by women who wanted heirs before?

She stroked her hood absently, imagining coming to Cored as the hopefuls came to Alex, watching his cock rise and his eyes go hot in arousal. Pilar arched her back, her breathing ragged. Would he drink from her body? What positions would he choose? The possibilities were staggering.

Her climax crested, and she sank back. The relief didn't last long. In moments, the ache returned, more powerful than the first time and more insistent. She needed Cored inside her.

He'll never break his vow.

Unless I tempt him. He said he'd finish anything I start with him.

Pilar didn't question that she would tempt him. She didn't even question why she would.

* * * *

Cored closed the door behind him, inhaling the glorious smell of roasted meat and tubers. By Mag, he could use a good meal. He turned from the door lock, and his stomach fluttered...but for a completely different reason.

Pilar sashayed toward him, dressed in a short bathing robe that covered only a hand-width of her thighs. There was no question in his mind that she was nude beneath it.

"Good evening," she greeted him with more than a hint of invitation in her tone.

"Good evening, Pilar." Was she trying to goad him into finishing? If so, she was well on her way.

She unbuttoned his jacket, pressing her lush, silin covered breasts to him as she pushed it away. The scent of iri surrounded her, mixed with the smell of fruit and musk...and something more that he couldn't name.

"Would you like some fruit before dinner?" she offered.

"Yes. I would." *And an explanation.*

He followed her to the kitchen, loosening his belt as his cock squeezed beneath it. Cored took his usual seat, his head spinning.

Pilar brushed a lizor berry over his lips, and he bit into it. He groaned as her flavor swirled through his mouth with that of the fruit.

Not just her flavor. Pilar painted her climax on it for me.

Mag as my vow-keeper, I am going to finish this.

A slice of implin followed. Cored didn't hesitate. The mixed flavors were divine. Another slice.

"You are tempting me, Pilar. I will finish this." It was only right that he should remind her what she was agreeing to by doing this.

Rather than answering him or shying away, she lifted her leg and swung it over his to stand astride his knees, uncovering her golden mound just long enough to convince him he'd been right about her state of undress. She brought another slice of implin up, hesitated then slid her hand through the slit of the robe and brought the implin slice out again, glistening with a fresh coat of her personal sucre.

Cored took it, sucking her juice and the fruits' off of her fingers. He released her and chewed slowly, considering this new temptress in her. It was disconcerting, but he enjoyed it.

She reached for more fruit, and he captured her hand, guiding it back to the slit of her robe. Pilar met his gaze, questioning him silently.

He grasped her hips, lifting her to the edge of the table. Pilar raised her legs, placing her feet on his knees. Then she spread the robe wide around her legs and leaned back on her elbows, offering him the taste he wanted. Cored parted his legs slowly, watching hers follow. Her feet slid further up his thighs as he moved toward her.

She gasped at the first stroke of his tongue up her slit. Her flavor was so sublime, he nearly echoed the noise. The slight sweetness of the fruit offset the tang of her climax.

"Are you hungry, Cored?" she asked.

"Famished." For every inch of her body.

Pilar licked her lips, nodding, trembling. Something wasn't right, but Cored couldn't name what it was. This wasn't like her.

She tipped her hips, urging him on silently...then noisily, as he feasted on the cornucopia of flavors she offered.

She arched her back, her hands fisting in the table cover. "I need you inside me," she pleaded.

Cored rose, looking for some explanation for her behavior. Pilar pressed to his body, wrapping her legs around him. She drew his mouth down to hers, kissing him in wild abandon...and the answer became clear.

He fisted one hand in her hair, guiding Pilar back. As he expected, her eyes were dilated. Cored grasped the cup next to a glazed pot, sipping the orange liquid inside with a wince and a curse.

Dolgen...uncut. It was at least twice as strong as he would have mixed it for himself.

Pilar unbuckled his belt.

"How much have you had?" he asked urgently. Len knew it wasn't just a cup. What she'd done had taken time, and she was in a frenzy for him still. "Pilar—"

She moved on to the buttons.

"Pilar! How much?"

Her smile was slow and lazy.

"Len be damned," he grumbled. She'd had more than she should, but how much was that?

Cored pulled the lid off the pot, gaping at the level, shivering at Pilar stroking his still-rigid length.

Think! Reason! Assuming the pot had been full when she'd started—*and, Mag willing, she hadn't made herself cupfuls before*—Pilar had at least three cups of the Dolgen tea. *Six, at that strength.* No matter how desperate he'd been to collect his fee from a noblewoman, Cored had never had more than four cups, and he was much larger than Pilar was.

She nipped at his jawline. "Cored," she panted out.

Her stroking became more purposeful, and he shivered in response.

"I'm offering, Cored. I'm tempting you."

But could he take advantage of this?

Her mouth ravaged the well of musk at his throat, nearly folding his knees in response. "I need you inside me, Cored."

Gods, but she would! In that dosage, Pilar would be in a mating frenzy for at least half the night.

Cored closed his eyes, fighting for clarity. If he took advantage of this, it would be dishonorable. In this state, she had no choice but to want completion. If he didn't do this, she'd be in physical pain when denied...the same pain he'd been in when Corin had refused him after a single sexual encounter the evening she'd learned she carried.

He opened his senses to her in desperation. "Do you want me to love you?" he asked, planning to let her emotions decide for him. If she wanted him, she'd have him. If she was confused or driven mindlessly, he'd seek a medical counteragent at the clinic instead. Gods help him, her family would believe he'd given her the drug himself.

"Just you, Cored. I've never wanted anything but this."

Her emotions were deep and heartfelt, unmuddied, something beyond want, beyond trust... Cored decided he didn't have a name for what she felt.

He sealed his mouth to hers, groaning as she pushed his trousers away and levered herself up to guide his cock head to her ready body. Cored leaned her over the tabletop and thrust into her.

Pilar pulled at his hips, rising to his advances, rocketing toward release...and over. He followed her, lost in the emotions he hadn't blocked. She screamed in delight, her hands fisting in his tunic as he locked into her band.

He stroked a hand along her cheek, marveling at how sensual and beautiful she was. Pilar sank to the table, her hand brushing over the cup in a clumsy bid to grasp it. Cored lifted it and drank it down, determined to sate her as often as she required until the Dolgen released her mind and drives.

His cock lessened, and he left her body, shivering as she whimpered a protest. The need assaulted her again...and him by association of their link.

"Turn off the meal," he rasped. "We'll eat it later."

She slid from beneath him and complied. Cored refilled the cup and gulped the Dolgen down, pouring the final cup before she turned from the oven. He drank it, his gaze locked with hers.

"I can make some more," she offered.

He set the cup on the table and strode to her, stripping off his tunic and dropping it to the floor. The burn of needing her ate at him, though he knew the Dolgen had yet to take effect.

Pilar met him halfway, her hands undoing the tie on her robe. Cored lifted her, fit her to his body, and headed for the bed.

There would be no more Dolgen. When the drug released her, he would dump the rest.

CHAPTER SEVEN

Jad 22, Ri 25-3016

Pilar licked her lips, moaning at the heady taste of musk in her mouth. She searched her memories, confused at awakening this way.

Her heart pounded at the crash of the truth through her reluctant mind. She'd seduced Cored. Pilar couldn't comprehend where the plan had come from...or where the decision to do it had.

She stroked herself, remembering preparing the fruit for him. His reaction had been captivating. All of his reactions had been...as far as she could remember.

The evening had been a haze of touching and tasting, promises and pleas. Her muddled mind insisted that the feast had lasted until well into the night, and they'd never returned to the kitchen for their aborted dinner.

"Fion have mercy," Cored breathed. He turned over her, holding himself up on one elbow. He grasped her wrist, bringing her hand to his mouth, licking their mixed fluids with an intense look.

Cored didn't ask her permission. She answered him anyway, a gasped 'yes.'

His cock eased past her swollen outer lips and into a body that ached in a combination of indescribable pleasure and sweet little pains of use. Cored took her gently, a slow assault on her bruised tissues and battered nerves.

"Fion, please," she begged. Already, climax closed on her.

"I can't get enough of you." Cored's lips pressed to her temple, a rough, impatient kiss punctuated by his cock forcing into the well-used band at the gates of her womb.

They cried out together, his fluids buffeting her contracting muscles, his cock forcing her gates wide so that the heat surged up and she released yet another egg. Then their mouths meshed, a hungry communion of bodies.

Their ardor eased as his erection did. Pilar stared at him, unable to put her rioting feelings into words.

Cored pressed his forehead to hers. "Please... Don't deny me."

She didn't consider her answer. "I won't."

* * * *

Cored winced as Pilar did. She'd been shifting uncomfortably on the chair since they'd started eating. He'd hoped the bath she'd taken while he heated the uneaten roast would ease her discomfort, but it hadn't.

Being accustomed to frequent sex, Cored wasn't actually uncomfortable. His cock was sensitized, easily brought to readiness, throbbing lightly at every touch.

He stroked his fingertips over the table, remembering their first time in startling detail. Pilar's gasp brought him back to reality. She was too sore for a repeat. *Unless...*

Her eyes widened as he stood and went to her. She turned to him, pressing her lips to his cock through his trousers. Cored cradled her head to him, wanting what no noblewoman had ever offered. Her breathing hitched, but she continued.

He forced his eyes not to close, licking his lips as she opened his trousers and eased his cock out. Pilar's blue eyes sought him out.

At first, he thought she was asking for direction or permission. Then her tongue flicked out, stroking the underside and circling the head very deliberately, testing his responses. She paused.

"Anything," he vowed. "I'll give you anything."

Her lips closed around the tip, and he laid his head back, closing his eyes. A strangled cry escaped his lips as she took him deeper in. Pilar experimented, learning his likes and dislikes. He teetered on the edge of release in moments, torn between the desire to have her finish him and the desire to have her band holding him tight again.

"I will repay this," he managed. He'd tasted her band. Now she'd taste him.

Pilar groaned, and the vibration set off his climax. A static charge raced up his length, and he pulsed in response, a spasmodic pleasure he'd rarely felt, no matter how sorely he'd been used. His fluids poured out, filling her mouth so that she swallowed reflexively. Then he was swelling, trapped between the roof of her mouth and her sweet tongue.

Cored's knees shook. He turned, half-sitting, half-falling to the table's surface, his hands fisted in her hair. Pilar moved with him, holding him captive inside her.

She released him abruptly, still hard. He roared in disbelief as she licked him again and again, maddening sensation at a time when he typically felt nothing but the stillness of the band. Pilar hesitated, and he bucked his hips, urging her on.

Her wicked tongue bathed him, caressing him as the swelling subsided. The stimulation kept him erect and wanting, which brought him back to his initial plan.

Cored drew her to her feet and stood, stroking his fingertip along her come-beaded lower lip. She sucked his finger in with a hungry look, no doubt aroused to a near frenzy by his musk and seed.

He turned around her, urging Pilar to the edge of the table, forcing her legs wide and laying her forward across it. She grasped the sides, bracing herself for a rough ride. Cored smiled at that.

Her skirt retreated behind his hands. He lowered himself to his knees, inhaling her ready scent greedily. If she was ready now, she'd climax in his mouth before he was through.

Her slit was swollen and an angry red. *As well it should be.* Pilar was unaccustomed to making love, and the six—or more, since his memories of the Dolgen-fired hours were sparse—times since he'd coupled with her the night before would have been akin to a trauma.

He pressed his lips to it and concentrated a burst of healing. She gasped, then sobbed, her scent intensifying. Cored healed her again, laying teasing licks on her now-pink tissues, and she pressed back into his hands.

"More?" he inquired, puffing air over her in a silent taunt.

"No."

"No?" He thought she would beg for more. Though the color had returned to normal, the swelling hadn't subsided.

"It..." She gasped again, her hands white-knuckling the table edge.

"The swelling... It feels good," he guessed.

"So good."

He flicked his tongue inside, smiling as she cycled her hips against him. "Tell me what you want, Pilar."

"Make love to me." It was the first time she hadn't used some crude euphemism for the act.

Cored pushed to his feet, lifting her fully onto the table so her feet left the floor and her slit was at his level. He spread her nether lips wide with his thumbs, waiting for her groan to continue.

He fit his cock head between, stilling just inside her body. Pilar wiggled against him, forcing him a finger-width deeper, arching up as he slid against her inner pleasure spot.

Their positions resonated with him, and Cored hesitated. This wasn't right. She'd asked him to make love to her. Was this how little he prized Pilar? He retreated slowly.

She sobbed as he left her body.

Cored gathered her into his arms and strode to the bedroom, settling her on her hands and knees. He spread her folds again and eased inside. "I believe we were here," he managed.

Pilar forced herself back until he felt the ridge of her pleasure spot. "No. Here."

He reached the gates of her womb in one long slide. "I prefer here."

She trembled, gasping out her agreement. Oh yes, deep inside her was the one place he needed to be.

His thrusts were slow and easy, though to the hilt at each pass. Pilar's gasps became pleas for more then a myriad of vocalizations of pleasure...followed by screams of release.

"I'm going to heal you, Pilar," he promised. "And when I'm drunk on our mixed fluids and you're aroused by my healing, I'm going to start making you sore again."

A second climax overlapped the first.

"You want that. Don't you? You want me to make love to you. Don't you?"

"Oh, yes." That was undeniably the truth.

CHAPTER EIGHT

Jad 23, Ri 25-3016

Cored opened his eyes, smiling at the feeling of Pilar wrapped in his arms. They'd spent the previous day in bed, emerging seldom...for necessities only. Even at that, midday meal had turned into a feast of touch and taste comparisons, and one trip to the bath had seen them using the tub for a much different reason than they'd initially intended.

Her feelings when she wasn't under the influence of the Dolgen were much the same as her feelings when she was. For that reason alone, the day had passed with as many encounters as the night before it had, without drugs to spur them on.

Given the feelings he knew she harbored for him and those he wasn't afraid to admit to himself that he had for her, there was only one possible answer. Cored had to offer a contract and hope she trusted him enough to accept its sincerity. *And accept me.*

Visions of days spent in a sensual haze had him hard again, but this wasn't the proper time for it. It was one of his usual clinic days, and he had to get ready.

Cored slid away from Pilar, hesitating as she stretched. The silin sheet slipped down her body, uncovering her breasts, pulling laces tight around his fast-beating heart. Pilar opened her eyes and sought him out, smiling in invitation.

His heart stuttered. "You'll be waiting when I return?" he asked.

"Why don't I come along?" she countered.

"What?"

"Noblewomen do offer time at the clinics."

He nodded, dumbstruck. *Why? You've always known she was gracious.*

That much was true, but most noblewomen who gave time at the clinics weren't gracious. They were self-serving: searching for reliable noble or gifted husbands or lovers, trying to appear less shallow or simply bored and hoping for a distraction. They all left when they found what they sought...or didn't.

"Oh... They won't let me, because I'm untrained." There was a note of disappointment in that.

Cored opened himself to her, confirming the emotion. With Pilar, it paid to be certain. "Each healer or doctor determines that for himself or herself," he assured her. "You can work with me...if you wish it." For some reason, the possibility of her refusal bothered him.

Pilar smiled, launching from the bed to wash and dress. Cored forced back his arousal. Just watching her backside sauntering to the cabinet was enough to floor him.

* * * *

Pilar handed a wet cloth to Cored, watching as he stroked the blood from the worker's hand tenderly. Cored murmured words of calming, assuring the barely-adult male that he would carry little more than a light scar in the end.

Her heart skipped merrily along. Beliefs about Cored, predicated on the stories people told about him, shattered, replaced by the image of a caring man.

In minutes, the worker was healed. The young man panted in relief from what must have been excruciating pain. Pilar bathed his forehead, offering a smile of encouragement. She used a fresh cloth to bathe his hand again, noting his muscles unclenching as she removed the last traces of blood.

"It will be weak for several days," she parroted the speech Cored had repeated four times that morning. "Use hot soaks every two hours for a day, at least. Rest it often for several more days."

"My thanks, Pilar Laes," the youth replied, using her offered hand to pull himself to his feet. He tipped his head to Cored. "And you, mi'lord."

Pilar looked to Cored as the man strolled away, her smile faltering at Cored's seeming concern. "What is it?" she asked.

"What you said to Rendel..."

"I should have let you give the instructions," she guessed.

His head shook slowly in disagreement, his gaze locked with hers. "No. I told you to do any little thing that didn't encompass healing, with my leave and thanks."

"Then what?" Surely, she'd done something wrong.

"Your attention and concern is touching. For patients and for me. You do so many little things that none of the others think to do."

Her cheeks heated in pleasure, though he'd offered only a simple observation. "I'll watch for more chances to do so," she promised.

He paused then nodded his encouragement.

* * * *

"Pilar Laes, how nice to see you."

She turned to the strange voice, noting the man's averted gaze with an easing of her heart. "Mi'lord?" *Oh, I hope this isn't another man who thinks I should know him.*

His gaze didn't stray her way. Instead, it meandered toward the serving line. Pilar followed his line of sight to Cored.

"Be cautious, Pilar Laes."

She examined his expression, taking inventory of features that were so similar to Cored's. "Are you his brother?" Based on his approximate age, it was a safe wager this was Cullin and not an uncle or other relative.

His jaw tightened, and he offered a curt nod. "Cored is dangerous. You should know that."

"Not without reason, in my estimation." Pilar fumed at this man's presumption.

Cullin raked his gaze up her body to her face. "He *has* a reason."

She crossed her arms over her chest, wary of another visual assessment by this man. "You believe Cored means to use me to regain position." If he was going to be rude and direct, Pilar was

75

more than capable of being blunt in return. She'd had years of dealing with her brothers to hone the skill.

"He did demand a Trial Moon, I've heard." There was something patronizing in that, as if Pilar was a child in need of his protection.

Great. Yet another man with that delusion. "Cored had no intention of it, if you must know. I suggested it...to give us more time to get to know each other." They'd certainly been doing that of late...in the bedroom and out.

Cullin sighed, and a sad little smile turned up one corner of his lips. "That's what Cored does, I'm afraid. He's...strange that way."

"What way?" she inquired, perplexed by his circumspect manner.

"People do things they can't explain at Cored's manipulation...at his touch."

Before she could recover from her shock, he was in motion toward the corridor doorway.

"Pilar?" Cored questioned.

She swiveled her head, considering him. Had Cored manipulated her? Every move had been her own, even that first night. Everything she knew of him debunked the idea that he was forcing her into decisions.

Out of the corner of her eye, she caught sight of Cullin's raised eyebrow. He was watching, waiting to see what she'd do next, perhaps hoping to see her treat Cored badly. There was little doubt that he hoped Pilar would believe him.

He kicked Cored out, disavowed him within days of his twentieth birthday... Now he was trying to alienate Pilar. Of course, Cullin would gain from

Cored being disavowed. The estate and other holdings would be Cullin's alone. Moreover, if Pilar accepted Cored, Cullin would lose by being forced to acknowledge his brother.

Cored's hand closed on her shoulder. "Pilar? What is it?"

She turned to him, aware that Cullin was watching.

If I do this, I'm encouraging Cored.

I want to encourage him. Pilar rose on tiptoe and brushed her lips over his, letting her eyes slip shut.

Cored hesitated, then pulled her toward him and deepened the kiss. There was nothing rushed in it, nothing frantic. He eased away with a sigh. Pilar opened her eyes, staring up at his expression of bliss with a lightening heart.

His eyes opened, and a smile pulled his lips up crookedly. "Ready to eat?" he asked in a roughened voice.

Pilar nodded, wondering where her voice had departed to.

Cored started to guide her chair out, stopped, then snapped his head up. His entire body stiffened, his eyes going hard. "Cullin," he breathed.

Pilar placed a hand on his arm, glancing toward Cullin's retreating back. "Cored... He's not worth it. Trust me. If I ever doubted it, I don't now."

His head turned toward her, and his eyes narrowed. "You knew he was there?"

She bit at her lower lip, sensing something was wrong. "Well, he... He had the nerve to..."

Cored raised an eyebrow, all but tapping his fingers on the table in impatience.

Pilar nodded, steeling herself for something she couldn't name.

"Len be damned," slipped from between his clenched teeth. He glared at her. "What were you thinking?"

"You were the one who said you'd—"

Cored straightened to his full height, darkening in what she'd assume was anger. "After I told you not to play that game with me, why would I play it with you? Or want you to play it with me again?"

"But you said—"

"This isn't a game, Pilar."

Her heart ached at his condemnation. She turned to go, fighting back tears. It was a full five steps before Cored reacted.

"Pilar?"

She shook her head and kept moving, praying to Fion that he wouldn't chase her down. She'd end up blubbering if he did that.

His hand closed on her shoulder. "Pilar...wait."

Her emotions rioted. Part of her wanted him to hold her, to apologize or at least say he knew she'd meant well. Another part wanted to escape him before the sobs she was swallowing down won.

His hand retreated. "I'm sorry," he whispered. "I didn't mean to hurt you."

Pilar nodded and hurried away.

She managed to hold her emotions in check until the clinic desk had summoned her a car, Pilar had been delivered to Cored's home, and she'd shut herself into the cottage. Then the tears flowed.

On some level, Cullin had been right. Nothing was a game to Cored. Forced to it or not, everything was serious; everything was planned. The man had no space for relaxation and laughter in his life. Nothing touched him...save his healing.

Miserable and aching, she retreated to the lounging couch in the library. It would be better to live the rest of the Trial Moon here.

CHAPTER NINE

Cored watched her go, his appetite fled to parts unknown. He'd hurt her, and Cored had no desire to do that.

He didn't have to question his anger, though he wondered at it. At some point, some murky moment since he'd met Pilar, his quest to force his brother to acknowledge him had become less important to him than Pilar was.

The idea that Pilar had played at his feelings—whether to provoke her brothers or his—ate at him. Cored wanted her passion to be real, not feigned in some game, even one he'd claimed he wanted to play with her. He'd been playing this game, in one form or another, for over a decade, but Pilar wasn't supposed to be part of the game.

Well, she was supposed to be part of it...originally. Why isn't she now?

He shook his head, at a loss to answer that to his own satisfaction.

It was real. Her emotions during and after the kiss had been sincere, no matter her thought process in initiating the kiss.

And now I've hurt her...again. At this rate, she'd never trust him, and Cored wanted her to trust him more than anything. He'd live happily in his little cottage, if Pilar was with him. Was his family's manor ever half the home he'd had with Pilar?

He knew it hadn't been. Why would he want to go back to it? Just to be welcomed, however grudgingly? Just to win in this battle against Cullin?

"It's not worth it," he breathed.

"Cored?"

He didn't turn to Administrator Azen. "Yes?" There was probably another case that would benefit from his healing magic.

"Your meal?"

His stomach cramped at the thought of eating it. "I don't seem to be hungry, after all."

"You've done quite a lot of healing today. I'll have someone drive you home."

Inspiration struck. "I'd appreciate a car, but not to home. I'd like to make a stop in town first."

"As you wish. I'll arrange it." He bustled away to call for a driver, and Cored ambled after him.

Convincing Pilar that he was sincere wouldn't be easy. To convince her, every disadvantage would have to be his.

* * * *

The cottage was so quiet and still, Cored panicked in the certainty that she'd left him. He padded into the semi-darkness, afraid to break the silence, visions of no response to his call killing the sound in his throat before he could issue the call to be ignored or unheard.

A rustling sound from the library set his heart on something resembling a normal rhythm. Cored moved to the doorway, searching out Pilar in the gloom.

She was lying in a loose ball on the lounging couch, buried beneath a quilt. Though he was certain she was awake, Pilar didn't react to his presence.

"I'm sorry, Pilar. I didn't mean to hurt you." He'd said it once, but it couldn't hurt to repeat it.

"Don't. You're right. It's not a game. I shouldn't have made it one." There was no emotion in that.

"And I shouldn't have overreacted to—"

"You didn't."

Cored sank to his knees beside her, reaching out to touch her shoulder. Pilar jerked away from him, settling on the floor across the couch from him.

"Pilar?" What had he done to warrant this reaction?

"I don't think we should..."

"I'm not trying to get you into my bed." Why would she think that? He suddenly wished he'd asked what Cullin had told her.

"Good." Her shoulders eased at that.

Good? Whatever was going on here, it made no sense. "Is it?"

Pilar nodded.

Cored fought for words then gave up on the discussion. There was little chance he'd settle this tonight. "It's late."

"I don't think I should—"

"I'm not talking about bed. Have you eaten?"

She hesitated a moment. "No."

He offered his hand, and she stared at it, seemingly wary. It was almost certain Cullin had told her Cored could control her by touching her. It wouldn't be the first time his brother had told that lie.

"It's too late to cook something. I'm only suggesting an inn."

Her features hardened. "I thought you didn't want to show off our—"

"I'm not. Besides, it's highly unlikely that Cullin will be at an inn in this part of town."

Pilar's expression slid from one emotion to another so quickly it was dizzying. "A meal," she agreed, as if she was compromising. If she was, Cored had no clue what she'd decided, but it didn't bode well for him.

* * * *

Pilar stared at her plate, her emotions rioting. How could she still want a man she'd argued she had no future with? Why was she playing with her heart this way? Reversing herself at every turn?

"I've been thinking about our situation," Cored stated.

Pilar stared at him, forcing herself not to gape like a child. *Our situation. Doesn't that say it all? It's not a relationship. It's a situation.* "So have I." How she managed a steady voice was beyond her.

He stirred his lamor in cream sauce absently. "You and I... We're good for each other, Pilar."

Sexually. She didn't answer.

"I think there may be...the possibility...of something more for us." He gave another stir to his food. "Something beyond the Trial Moon, if you'd like that." There was something hesitant in that.

"If I'd like that?" Wouldn't he like it? Was it to be a contract of convenience? One of those awful contracts of alliance?

"We don't have to sign the Trial Moon contract, you know. If we agree to something different..." He waited for her to respond, his muscles strung tight as if in readiness for a fight.

Her heart ached. Pilar wasn't blind to the fact that she wanted him; she'd always wanted him, but was it enough to tie herself to Cored? She'd always said sex wasn't what she wanted from him, but sex with Cored was admittedly fantastic. If a contract with him meant the life she'd led with him the last few days, would it be enough?

"Pilar?"

"I..." *Is it enough?* Until she could answer that question, she didn't dare commit to anything more. "I don't know what I want, Cored." That was true.

His shoulders drooped; then he stiffened. He offered a curt nod of his head. "We'll discuss it another time."

"That would be best," she agreed.

There was a moment of silence, bringing a tension she'd thought had evaporated between them. Pilar took a sip of her wine, noting that Cored was busy pushing his meal around the plate instead of eating it.

"Pilar?"

She took a calming breath. "Yes?"

"When we get home..."

Home. Pilar had started to think of his home as her own.

Belatedly, she realized what he was asking. Was she willing to share his bed?

Answering that wasn't difficult. No matter what she decided about a contract—*either contract*—there was no denying Pilar wanted more of Cored. When all was said and done, this month with him might be all there was for her.

"I think bed is a good idea, Cored. Just remind me to bring the quilt from the lounging couch back to the bedroom with us."

A smile flirted with his lips. "I'll collect it for you."

CHAPTER TEN

Jad 29, Ri 25-3016

Pilar rubbed at her forehead, closing her eyes. She was pregnant...and still no closer to an answer than she'd been nearly a week earlier.

At times, she was certain there was more between them than an enjoyable shared bed. At others, Cored was so moody, she hardly recognized him. He was so tense at every indication that more might lie between them, she was reminded of her realization that there was no room for games and frivolity in his life.

And now there was a child to consider.

Pilar settled her head on her crossed arms, completely unmotivated to make herself a tea with olum, though it would ease her pregnancy signs. She sighed in the realization that she'd be forced to drink redroot tea, unless she wanted to go to the marketplace.

And I don't.

The lizor berry tea had run out the day before, and she hadn't mentioned to Cored that it was gone. Worse, the fragrant orange tea she enjoyed so much was an import of some sort. Cored had accidentally spilled the remaining tin into the wash water, and it was difficult to find in the marketplaces, he attested.

The aches aren't going to go away on their own. That a given, she forced herself to her feet and started water boiling for the redroot tea.

The babe isn't going away, either. That prompted another sigh, and Pilar paused, the spoon halfway inserted into the tin of tea.

There would be a contract now. Whether she signed Cored's contract or accepted the terms of the Trial Moon contract, there was no question she'd have to sign some manner of agreement with him.

But I can dissolve the contract.

If she dissolved the Trial Moon, the babe would be her own, and she knew precisely how much money she'd owe him to escape a more formal arrangement with him. It would be a lot of money, enough to make Cored fantastically rich, in comparison to his current standard of living, but there was no fear of him taking the babe from her.

Pilar had no idea what Cored's contract would say. Every time he'd offered to discuss a contract with her, she'd shied. In the end, Pilar had to admit she was something of a coward. She was so afraid that it would be a contract of alliance, she wasn't willing to hear it and be disappointed again.

And I don't know what stipulations he'd want for children.

I won't know if I don't ask. That was one thing she couldn't deny.

If I ask, and his contract is untenable, there is still the Trial Moon contract. He couldn't refuse her right to choose it, and it favored her.

Pilar wove her way back to the table, her head spinning. It was always like this when she considered the problem of the contracts.

A knock sent her veering away from the table and toward the door. She smoothed her dress, then her hair, just in case it was one of her brothers. Though they rarely ventured to Cored's home—*probably afraid of what I'll do to annoy them*—it was possible, and the last thing she needed was for them to think she was ill...or being mistreated. Len only knew what they'd do to Cored if they believed that.

It wasn't a family member, but it was a royal messenger with an invitation for her to attend the celebration of her older brothers' birthdays at the palace. Pilar sent the messenger off with a promise to answer at her earliest convenience. Then she returned to the kitchen to finish making the tea.

If it was any event but one for her immediate family, she'd probably beg off. As it was, she would have to go. The question was whether to take Cored along or not.

Wake up. The celebration is the least of your worries. What are you going to do about the contract? The pregnancy? Cored and the rest of your life?

Pilar groaned, burying her face in one shaking hand. Whatever she did, she needed olum and a hot bath before making the decision.

* * * *

Cored ambled through the door, his tunic untied and cuffed to his elbows. He cursed the heat inside the cottage. It would cool after the sun went down, but until then, it would be stifling.

The winter systems in the cottage were exemplary, but the cooling had never worked properly.

Would it be worth selling yourself another five times to install a working one? The answer to that was obvious. It wasn't. That was why he'd never done so.

But now there was Pilar to consider. He winced in the realization that she had to be uncomfortable in this sauna.

As if in denial of that belief, the lady in question sauntered down the corridor, dressed in a bathing robe, red-faced but smiling. She rose on tiptoe, wrapping her arms around his neck.

Cored grimaced at the heat radiating off of her. "We have to get you into a cool bath."

Pilar shook her head. "I just took a hot one."

On inspection, her hair was damp. Cored fingered it. "Why hot?"

"If the water is hotter than the room..." She left the rest unsaid.

"Strange. I've never tried that."

She nipped at his chin. "Maybe we can try one together...after we eat."

"You're hungry?" He never was, while the sun was up at the height of summer.

Pilar nipped harder. "In more ways than one."

His cock rose as her meaning became clear. Cored started guiding her toward the bed. "First we make love," he informed her.

"Then the bath," she continued.

"Then we slake other hungers." By then, the sun would be down.

Pilar untied her robe and slipped it off, then went work on his trousers. Cored half-stumbled after her, planting his hand on the bedside table to keep from falling over her on the mattress.

The shift of paper brought his gaze down. "A missive?" he asked.

She pulled up at his tunic. "An invitation. We're going."

Cored dragged the tunic off. "Going?"

"To the palace for my brothers' birthday party."

He groaned. "They won't—"

"I don't care what they want." Pilar pushed his trousers away, tugging at the waistband to urge Cored to the bed.

"It's their celebration."

"No, it's a celebration *for* them," she corrected. She pushed lightly, toppling Cored to the mattress.

"Pilar, if we do this, people will say I'm flaunting our—"

His protest died in his throat as Pilar climbed astride him, impaling herself on his cock. She levered herself up his length then down again.

"There are three reasons you're going to attend with me."

"I'm listening," he gasped. Cored couldn't promise how much he'd retain of what she said, but it was safe to say Pilar had his full attention.

"First." She performed the same slow glide up and down his length. "My family will expect to see us together."

He nodded, rapt on the way her breasts shimmied with every downward slide of her sheath around his cock. What she was saying made sense, so far. *I think.*

"Second." Another torturous glide. "We haven't had a chance to dance together, and you will dance with me at the celebration."

"Oh, yes." He'd dance with her. Cored could imagine Pilar in his arms for an Earth-style dance already.

"Third." Pilar rotated her hips, clenching her inner muscles down tight on his length. "I am going to make it very worth your while to attend."

He stared at her, working at that. "Worth my—"

She started driving herself up and down on him. "Is this worth—"

Cored flipped her beneath him, thrusting hard and fast. "You are worth anything you ask, Pilar, but you don't have to bribe me."

The move forced her to a kinetic climax, and Cored followed her. They lay together, sweat-soaked, sticky, exchanging slow, deep kisses.

"We'll go," he breathed.

Her legs circled his waist. "I'm not bribing you. I want you."

Cored took a moment to search out her emotions, his lessening cock aching for more. "You've got me. In the tub," he grumbled.

"Then on the table," she teased.

CHAPTER ELEVEN

Caj 7, Ri 25-3016

Pilar smiled at Cored across the ballroom. He was perfectly at home at the palace, entertaining Pyter with sleight of hand.

"I wouldn't have thought a re-bred like you would need him," a cold female voice commented.

Pilar looked around in surprise, her gaze settling on Corin's twisted smile. "Excuse me?" she asked, trying to summon the mask that would say she cared what the beast was going on about.

Corin raised an eyebrow. "The former Cored Li?" She fanned manicured nails before her face, her gaze settling on Cored with a hungry look that turned Pilar's stomach. "I certainly wouldn't mind sharing my bed with him again. The man knows how to use his staff."

"I have no idea what you're—"

"Of course you do," Corin dismissed her. "But why would you pay a man to have a child? Any man—even a blessed one—would contract to a child with you, probably for less than what you'd pay Cored for more than a few weeks or any man for a Trial Moon."

Pilar's stomach lurched, the vision of Cored fucking Corin taking unwelcome residence in her mind. The rest of Corin's speech filtered in. "You *paid* Cored to...to have sex with you?"

"Of course. The man does produce lovely children." Corin scowled. "Mine was male. Maybe

I'll arrange to try again for a female." Her smile returned. "You know he's worth every coin."

The room suddenly seemed too close, the air too thick. Pilar closed her eyes, trying to find her emotional center. Corin continued, shattering Pilar's illusion of peace.

"I never brought him out to functions. I don't think I left bed for more than six hours at a time the entire three weeks it took to conceive my—"

"Why are you here, Corin?" Pilar snapped. "I thought you gave up on palace parties after Joseph chose Berel over you." She met Corin's eyes, hoping for pain at the reminder.

Corin didn't seem pained. She didn't even seem embarrassed by the reminder. The 'lady' looked across the room with another hungry expression. "There are other men," she noted.

Pilar followed her line of sight, expecting to see Cored, but Corin was looking past Cored to Alex. "I wouldn't lay wagers," Pilar growled, making a mental note to warn Alex that Corin was on the hunt for his attentions. Not that Alex needed her assistance in rebuffing women.

"Oh really? Why is that?" She didn't seem concerned by the warning; she hardly seemed to notice it.

"Alex has better taste. He prefers to do his duty with commoners. After all, you can afford to buy a child. They can't." Pilar stormed away before Corin recovered from her shock enough to speak. It had been an incredibly rude statement, but if anyone deserved it, Corin did.

Pilar didn't pause. She knew where she was headed. She and her brothers had been raised with Jole and Susan's children. Pilar had climbed the grain well, played in the King's Corridors, and explored every room of the massive palace in her youth. The library had always been her favorite place to think, to escape crowds, and to calm from any upset.

She looked back in surprise as the door closed, stilling with her hand on a Keen history she cared for. Pilar scowled at her unwanted pursuer. "Go away, Loryol." She didn't bother to call him Loryol Li, when it was clear there was little lord-like about him.

"You're upset," he noted.

"Of course I am. You're here. Weren't you warned to stay away from me?" She knew he was, and it was a veiled warning, at best. If she called for Alex and Andrew, it was a safe bet Loryol would spend another few days in a cell.

"I was." Surprisingly, that didn't seem to concern him.

"Then go away."

"I can't apologize if I'm not in the same room you are."

Pilar rolled her eyes. "You've offered an apology. I really don't—"

"No. I haven't. Not a proper one." Loryol strode toward her.

Pilar ducked away, trying to put a chair between them and finding herself blocked from her goal by his larger body.

"If you touch me, I'll scream," she warned him. If she screamed, a cell would be the least of his worries.

Loryol put up his hands in a calming gesture, sinking to one knee. "I was wrong. I was so overjoyed that you accompanied me— That's not an excuse," he was quick to add. "I'd like the chance to prove I'm not the man you think I am."

She turned away, shaken. That was all Cored had asked from her. "I-I can't. Cored—"

"You don't seem very happy with Cored." There was something in that...collusion or perhaps an attempt at comfort.

Pilar looked back in surprise. Was she that easy to read? "Regardless, I gave my word." For the next six days, she was tied to Cored. Then he could have his blasted freedom. Her heart ached at that.

Loryol's head snapped up, and his eyes narrowed. "You haven't contracted with him, have you?"

* * * *

Cored held his breath, his fist pressed hard to the door frame. He'd known something was wrong when Pilar stormed from the ballroom. He hadn't expected this.

Pilar hesitated, looking hopelessly unhappy. It was a testament to her preoccupation that she hadn't noted him easing the door open to gauge the situation.

Her face hardened in a look Cored knew well but hadn't seen in weeks. "Of course not," she snapped.

Cored's stomach turned at the ice in her voice. He fought for a decent breath. How could he be so wrong about Pilar?

Loryol nodded. "Allow me the chance to make up for my atrocious behavior?"

She looked away to the window, seemingly considering it. "I don't think so, Loryol."

Cored breathed a sigh of relief. It was short-lived...only as long as it took for Loryol to stand and scoop her hand up in both of his.

Pilar startled. "You said—"

Cored tensed to move against Loryol.

"Whatever agreement you have with Cored is immaterial. If it's a child you want, my genetics are sound...in the low ninetieth percentile. I'll admit I don't possess the healing magic. No one below ninety-five does." He stepped closer to her. "You don't need Cored to—"

Pilar blanched. "I don't need you, either." She pulled her hand from his and wiped it on her skirts as if wiping off the memory of his touch. "I don't need any man who brings his genetic tests to bed as a bargaining bit."

Loryol glared at her. "And what is it that Cored brings to bed?" he demanded.

Pilar struck him across the cheek, her eyes flashing in fury. Loryol grabbed her by the arms, and Cored launched through the doorway. Loryol looked away from Pilar, releasing her a heartbeat before Cored knocked him off his feet with a punch to his unprotected abdomen.

Cored stepped between them. "What I bring to this engagement is my rights under a Trial Moon," he growled. "Ordinarily, I would turn you over to

Pilar's father, but it is my right to take this out of your hide. I should kill you for this and offer assurances."

He ground his teeth at the rules Jole Ri had set for these occasions. After the attack on Princess Jenneane, weapons were only granted to chosen guards and re-bred families. Cored wasn't a member of the Braeden family and was, therefore, unarmed. He fisted his hands, ready to beat Loryol to death.

Pilar touched his shoulder with shaking fingers. "Don't," she breathed. "Hurt him. Turn him over to my father, but don't kill him."

Cored opened himself to her emotions, grimacing at the stark terror in her. Was she afraid of him or of seeing him kill someone? "As you wish."

He dragged Loryol to his feet and propelled him toward the open doorway, smirking as the lord stumbled over his own feet and landed on his face on the carpet. Cored strode to him and dragged Loryol up again, applying pressure to the base of his skull as he pushed him toward the corridor.

"You will learn your place, Loryol," he growled. "You will never touch Pilar again. You have my vow on that."

Loryol rallied his strength, turning on Cored. Cored was prepared for that move. Loryol landed one blow, but the next two went to Cored.

Hands dragged Cored off the downed man before he could strike again. He put up his hands for peace, lest he would take blows from whoever was interfering.

The guard captain between them motioned a stand-down to his men. "Are you in need of assistance, Loryol Li?" he asked, without taking his gaze off Cored.

Cored rolled his eyes at that. After ten years, he should have expected the guard to accuse him. He'd let himself become complacent, comfortable in his surroundings...because of Pilar.

"Captain," Pilar called out in a shaky voice.

His eyes swiveled to take her in, and he paled. "Pilar Laes, are you well?"

"Thanks to Cored, I am. Would you be kind enough to deliver Loryol to my father for judgment?"

The captain shot Cored a look of suspicion. "Do you require a woman healer, mi'lady?"

Cored bristled at that, but Pilar spoke before he could.

"I am well, Captain. Please take Loryol and leave me."

He nodded. "If you would come with me, Cored—"

"I said to leave," Pilar growled. "Cored isn't going anywhere. He's not the one at fault here."

"But...Pilar Laes—"

"Assure my father that I am with Cored and in good health, if you please." It wasn't a request.

The captain nodded. "As you wish." He motioned another guard to pull Loryol to his feet. They left, guiding Loryol before them.

Cored closed the door behind them, not daring to look Pilar in the eye. "Are you well? Did he hurt you?"

"No. I'm fine."

He nodded, still hurting from her comment about contracting with him.

"Cored, I'm...sorry for the way they treated you."

"Don't be. It's the life I lead."

"It shouldn't be."

He turned to her. Pilar sat on the arm of a wide chair, looking miserable.

"Why did you leave the ballroom?" he asked. "It wasn't to meet Loryol, was it?" He'd wager against it, but nothing was sure. Cored had turned from the young prince and seen nothing but Pilar striding through the double doors to the back corridors with Loryol close behind.

Her eyes widened, and patches of color lit in her cheeks. "You think I'd willingly—"

"You didn't seem so adverse to his attentions, before he brought his genetics into it."

She stood, her jaw clenching in fury and her color rebounding to a high point. "I left the ballroom after a very interesting and enlightening discussion with one of your *friends*. You do remember Corin, of course."

Cored winced at more than a few unwelcome memories about the 'lady' in question. "Corin was never a friend. I'm not entirely uncertain that Corin isn't one of Len's servants." He paused then added the rest in a muttered voice. "If the gods are kind, she's got a place reserved in His dungeons."

"That didn't stop you from bedding her. She wants another go...a female child this time, if you please."

"It's no different than what your brother does," he reasoned. She may not approve of Alex's chosen service, but it didn't kill her kind feelings for him. *As if women are ever that balanced when it's a man they're sleeping with?* He pushed that thought away before it could make him heartsick.

"It's very different," she shouted. "Women don't pay Alex to give them heirs."

"Alex doesn't need the money. I do. My stipend for healing at the clinics doesn't stretch very far. Even with a modest living, I need a little more...sometimes. What other marketable talents do I possess? I was raised a *lord*, Pilar. My genetics...they're strong. Everything I have comes from them, in one way or another."

She rubbed at her neck, tears pooling on her golden lashes. "So that's why you assumed an heir was all I wanted? Because it's all other women want?"

"None of them did want anything more...except you. Mag help me! Every time I think I know what you want, I'm wrong."

"I told you long ago, I only wish for things I can't have." A cynical edge crept into her voice. "Maybe I should settle for an heir. When you have your freedom, I'd have something besides memories. You'd have enough money to save you from Corin for decades, and... It's not like I can trust any man on Kegin, even those I'm related to."

Cored stalked to her, determined to make himself clear. Either she'd accept his contract or not. He cupped her cheek, drawing her face up to his, his brow furrowing at the chill of her skin, even with a hearty blush. Was she ill? "Pilar..."

She pulled away from him, shaking her head. "Don't you understand? I don't want sex from you. I've never wanted that."

He pulled her to his chest, feathering his lips over hers. "That's not what I'm offering," he whispered.

Pilar met his lips urgently, parting to him...her skin heating against his until it seemed to burn against his hand and lips.

Cored jerked away, his mind working fast. He met her gaze, his mouth going dry in shock. "Merciful Mother. Why didn't you tell me?" He took a step back, glancing to the lush plane of her stomach in awe. His child rested there. It was glorious.

She turned and stormed to the door, breaking the spell. Pilar glanced back at him. "Because I wanted something more. You'll have your freedom tomorrow. I have no right to take any more of your time."

No. It isn't supposed to happen this way. He hadn't even had a chance to offer his contract. But, if he did it now, before she left him, she'd know he'd intended it before he knew. She'd never believe him otherwise. "Pilar, wait."

But she was gone, fleeing down the corridor and out of his life.

Cored raced after her, shouldering people out of his way with muttered apologies. He was only a few steps behind her when Pilar reached her older brothers.

Andrew took one look at the tears streaming down her face and stepped between them, bringing his dagger up in silent warning.

Cored halted with a curse. "Step aside, Andrew. This isn't what you think."

"I don't care what it is."

Alex eased Pilar to his chest, smoothing her hair. "What is it?" he asked.

"Just take me home," she requested.

Alex looked at Cored, confused and seemingly working his way through the laws governing their situation. "Home?"

Cored ground his teeth, noting the guards moving toward them and the crowd moving away from the possibility of an armed encounter. "You have to talk to me, Pilar. A Trial Moon doesn't end this way."

"It can," she sobbed. "It often does."

"It doesn't have to," he pleaded. "Neither of us wants it to."

She cast a tortured look his way. "We don't want the same things out of a contract either."

The guards stopped, forming a ring just far enough away to allow whispered exchanges to escape their hearing but close enough to move, if needed.

"You don't know that. You've never asked what I want."

"We know what you want," Andrew grumbled.

Cored scowled at him, biting back the urge to make his adversary eat that dagger. "You wish you did. Stay out of this. It's between Pilar and myself."

"She's requested our aid. That makes me a part of it."

"No," Pilar corrected him. "I requested you to escort me home, not to fight my battles or live my life."

"Pilar," Alex began, shooting a pained look at Cored, but pained for who wasn't clear. "By the rules of Trial Moon—"

She blanched. "We'll sign the contract tomorrow, and then I'll dissolve it." Pilar rubbed at an ache in her temple, the headache she hadn't told Cored she had.

"Please, Pilar," Cored whispered desperately. "Let me heal your pregnancy signs." It was a simple intimacy, one he'd dreamed of being blessed with. Not to mention, with Pilar in his arms, he could offer the contract he'd intended to earlier, whether she believed him or not, and gauge her emotional responses.

Andrew looked over his shoulder, his shock at the idea melting into something resembling pity.

Pilar averted her eyes. "No. I don't think... Please, just take me home."

Alex nodded. "If that's what you want."

Andrew offered Cored a curt nod. "Midday tomorrow at the estate," he offered gruffly.

Cored nodded. "I'll be there."

Andrew waited for Alex to lead Pilar away before he sheathed his dagger and turned to follow. The guards held position, as if Cored might attack the young lord's back.

Cored fingered the envelope in his jacket pocket. "This isn't over yet," he promised solemnly.

Andrew shot him a wary look, and the guards moved a step closer, placing him outside the ring. "That's Pilar's choice."

"Yes. It is," he conceded.

CHAPTER TWELVE

Caj 8, Ri 25-3016

Pilar looked up as Cored strode into the room. He had dressed in his best: a silver silin tunic, black trousers, polished boots and the deep blue jacket with silver trim that announced his healing magic. She smoothed the skirt of her day dress, feeling underdressed for the occasion.

Cored bowed his head to her. "Pilar. Are you well?"

She nodded. "Alex has been offering..." She didn't want to mention his healing. That brought memories of the time they'd shared at the clinic and of how Cored used his own healing to heighten their sex life. Pilar didn't need reminders like that.

He turned to Alex without hesitation, apparently having mastered telling the identical twins apart without them opening their mouths. "My thanks, Alex."

"My pleasure," her brother noted uncomfortably.

Her father cleared his throat, laying a contract on the desk before him. "If we could get this over with," he hinted.

Cored snagged the contract off the surface and scanned his gaze over it. He met Pilar's gaze. "This is what you want from me?"

She swallowed a sob and forced a jerking movement of her head to nod. It wasn't what she wanted. It never had been, but this would seem to be the best of several bad choices.

"You told me once that you never get what you want."

Her stomach seized in apprehension. "Cored—"

He ripped the contract in half and pitched it into the fire. "I won't sign that."

Pilar stared at him in disbelief while the room erupted in confusion.

"Why you dirty *bastard*," Andrew exploded. "By the laws of Trial Moon, you have no choice but to—"

"You made a vow," her father spoke over him.

"You don't want me?" she whispered. Any concept she'd had of a broken heart was rendered impotent, when compared to this situation.

Her family fell silent. Andrew glared at Cored, and Alex gripped his twin's arm to stop the brute from doing something illegal.

Cored stepped toward her, dropping to his knees before her. He wiped a tear from her cheek, sighing. "I want you, but I won't sign that contract."

"I don't...understand," she hitched out, cursing herself for the reaction.

He placed a kiss on her lips, and Alex jerked back on Andrew before his younger twin could launch at them to stop Cored from doing it. Pilar opened her mouth to question the move then closed it again, hopelessly lost. Cored pulled an envelope from the inside pocket of his jacket and placed it in her lap, motioning to it.

Pilar fumbled it open, looking at the contract inside without comprehension. "What is this?"

"I have spent the last month trying to convince you that I love you. Somehow...I haven't been able to do that. Whether you want me or not, we are signing this contract."

"You have no right to demand any more than a ritual contract," Andrew growled.

"Stay out of this," Cored warned him. To Pilar, he added a gentle admission of, "He's right, of course. Read the contract. Just read it."

Pilar forced her mind to attend to the verbiage set to paper. She shook her head. "You can't sign this," she breathed.

"I already have. More than two weeks ago. The magistrate witnessed it. Look at the date, Pilar."

"But...this says..."

Cored chuckled. "I know what it says. I want nothing from you...nothing but you. Not money. Not a title. Not a claim on our child or your estate. If that isn't enough to convince you, I don't know what I can do to—"

Pilar threw her arms around his shoulders, laughing as Cored landed on his back beneath her. "You'd really do this?" she asked.

"I've already done it. All you have to do is sign it, and it's binding."

"We'll come up with a new contract," she offered. "I can't sign this."

A sly smile turned up one corner of his lips, and he raised an eyebrow. "And insult me by offering me money and security? If you want me, that's enough. What is you want, Pilar? If you could have anything?" His eyes darkened in arousal.

Pilar blushed in response. "You."

"Then sign the contract. That's all you have to do."

She nodded. "I need a pen."

Pilar laughed aloud as three pens bobbed before her, held by the three older male members of her family.

* * * *

Caj 9, Ri 25-3016

Pilar let out a squeal and escaped the room, bolting for the library, Cored in pursuit. He caught her halfway down the corridor, tickling her to the floor, smiling at her flailing and laughing.

Her skirt slid up, revealing half the length of her pale thighs. The tickling forgotten, Cored skated his fingers beneath the silin, pushing it higher.

Her gasp drew his gaze to her face. Her color was high from their play but also in her rising arousal. Pilar's eyes pleaded with him for more, and her skin heated in her schen.

Their positions resonated with him. "In the bed—"

"No." She grasped a handful of his tunic and pulled Cored over her.

He groaned at the contact. "Pilar, please—"

"Here. Everywhere. In my father's gardens again."

The suggestion stole his ability to form words.

Pilar's legs circled his buttocks, drawing him into the cradle of her body. "There...in the clearing. I want to finish, Cored."

"Oh, yes." He reached to free his cock. "But here first."

The knock at the door interrupted her answer. A groan escaped her lips.

"It has to be Andrew. *Gawds*, but he has the worst timing."

Cored sighed. "If we don't let him in, he'll just break the lock."

"Then he deserves what he sees," she insisted stubbornly.

"No. Our passion is no one's game or entertainment or even rub but our own."

She nodded and released him, straightening the skirt over her thighs. Cored pushed to his feet and lifted Pilar after him, just in time for the second knock.

Pilar rushed to the door, opening it halfway with a sigh. The door stopped, and she moved her hand to brace it against someone seeking entry, stiffening. Cored didn't question her; he guided Pilar behind him, then stepped to the door.

The sight of Cullin made his mouth go dry. Cored didn't welcome him. Forcing coherent speech was difficult enough, let alone specific words. He'd lived in this cottage for nearly ten years, and Cullin had never come to see him.

Pilar wrapped her arms around Cored and pressed to his back. In a lightning flash, Cored knew precisely why his brother had come. It had been the expected outcome, after all.

Cullin found his voice first. "I suppose I'm not welcome then."

"I'm not uncivilized, but I demand that visitors to my home act likewise." If Pilar's reaction was any indication, she was stressed enough by Cullin's presence alone, and he'd yet to say or do anything offensive.

Beside that, Cored would be Len-damned before he'd allow Cullin to say he'd turned his brother away without hearing him out, ever the rogue.

"Of course, brother." Cullin offered a courtly bow for show.

Cored backed off and let him pass, waving the way to the library. When Cullin was out of sight, he turned to Pilar. "Would you rather wait in our room?" he offered. "I can tell Cullin you require an afternoon rest."

She smiled weakly. "No. Whatever he says, I intend to stand as witness." She placed her hand to his lips, cutting off his protest. "Cored...I love you."

His heart melted that quickly. Cored kissed the palm of her hand, then guided it to his bent arm, escorting her into the library.

Cullin, predictably, had taken a seat on the lounging couch, making certain that Cored and Pilar couldn't sit together. Cored led her to the chair and stood at her side.

"Is there a reason for your visit, Cullin?" He wanted to hear him say it, though he wasn't sure what answer he would give, in the end.

Cullin looked around, his face twitching as if he was biting back a grimace. "Come home, Cored."

"I am home." He didn't consider that. His family's manor had never felt half the home his little cottage did with Pilar here.

His brother ground his teeth in frustration. "You're a lord, Cored. You—"

"You want me back?" He knew Cullin didn't, but he wanted to see how far his family would go.

Cullin's jaw tightened down another notch. "Yes. We're accepting you back."

But you don't want *me back.* Cored had known they wouldn't. At least they weren't letting him down.

"This cottage is quaint, but it's not a manor."

Pilar leaned toward him, her face hard in fury. "If we wanted to live in a manor, we'd live with my family," she snapped. "Or I'd request one of my own."

Cored placed a hand on her shoulder, offering her a smile. He turned to Cullin. "I'm not a lord, Cullin. I don't want to be one, and Pilar seems to like it that way. Disowning me was the best thing you could have done. I live to please no one but myself and my bride now. The concerns of the nobility are no longer mine."

"Be reasonable, Cored. You can't possibly support children in this...place."

"We will manage."

They'd do better than manage. Though Cored had refused money and position, Pilar was still a titled lady and retained her fortune. They already had plans to move to a larger cottage with more bedrooms, and they'd retained two day servants to handle cooking and cleaning for Pilar.

Cullin stood, his face darkened. "You're refusing us? You're refusing your family?"

Cored laughed heartily, raising Pilar's hand to kiss her knuckles. "No, Cullin. I'm embracing my family...in a manner that makes us happy."

"This is your final word on the matter?"

He glanced at Pilar, noting her nod, then stared his older brother down. "Without a doubt."

Cullin didn't ask again. He stomped to the door and slammed it behind him.

Pilar stood, making her way to the empty corridor. "He really is a *jagoff*, isn't he?"

Cored smiled at the English euphemism. "I don't know what that is, but I imagine it's accurate."

She shifted from foot to foot nervously. "If you want a manor, I can petition for one of our own," she offered. "You could have a title...if you want one. I never asked you to give that up, you know."

He stared at her in amazement. Pilar would give him anything he asked for, everything he'd sacrificed to prove he loved her.

Cored reached for her, tickling her mercilessly, until Pilar was gasping beneath him, tears in her eyes. He looked down at her, his heart light. "You're offering me anything I want, Pilar, but all I want...is you."

Her arms slipped around his neck. "We'll still be visiting my father's—"

He captured her mouth, their groans mingling.

SECTION TWO:
Jearsen

A Matter of Perception

CHAPTER THIRTEEN

Endl 6, Ri 25-3017

"Have you ever seen such a pitiful display?" Gibril asked.

Eve forced a smile to her face. Gibril was the most obnoxious relative she had, the least palatable person Eve knew in general. "Some of them are rather sweet."

"Sweet?" She laughed heartily at that. "My dear cousin, men are not intended to be sweet. If they are not spice and fire, between the sheets and out, they are nothing."

Eve wrinkled her lightly-freckled nose at that. If she'd meet a man that made her think of spice and feel the burn, it would be by Fion's hand alone.

"Care for a dance, Hir?" a voice asked.

So much for the safety of the dais. Eve took a calming breath, smiled, and turned to accept his offer. Even the company of hopefuls was preferable to spending time with Gibril.

The words stuck in her throat. The lord before her met her eyes for only a moment, then averted his respectfully, leaving Eve aching for the lost connection. A wild buzzing coursed over her nerves, making her heart race.

Gibril snorted rudely, and her suitor darkened, mumbling his apologies, shifting as if to turn away.

"I would love to dance," Eve offered hurriedly, extending her hand toward him.

He looked up in seeming surprise, and Eve's bodice abruptly felt two fingers too tight. His hand enfolded hers, and he steadied her down the stairs.

It took a moment for the odd shifting of his arm as they made their way to the dance floor to draw her gaze down. Realization came slowly. He walked with a limp.

Eve's wonder at it was cut short. Half swallowed chuckles from a group of lords turned to outright laughs and stage-whispered comments about 'the upstart cripple.' Eve shot them a quelling look that only succeeded in quieting them the slightest degree.

At the edge of the dance floor, she turned to him, noting his discomfort in anger. How dare those lords make a guest uncomfortable in her home!

"If you would rather not..." he offered sheepishly.

Eve squeezed his hand. "You promised me a dance," she reminded him. *But his limp...* "Would you be offended if I requested a Human dance?"

His smile was bright and heartfelt; he raised her hand from his arm to his chest in answer. "Whatever you wish." His voice was dark and full of promise yet not the bold presumption of the more annoying of the hopefuls.

She pressed her other hand to his chest then fit her body to his, smiling shakily as he wrapped his arms around her waist. Seeing her intent, the musicians cut the Keen music short and opened with her mother's favorite love song from Earth.

The snickering died out as they started to move together, the swaying and shuffling of the Human dancing masking his disability perfectly, just as she'd hoped it would.

"Thank you," he whispered.

Eve met his eyes, confused by his words of gratitude.

"You could have refused," he continued.

"So could you," she countered.

* * * *

Jearsen's surprise melted into a pressing need to laugh. He bit it back, trying not to offend Eve Hir. Her twinkling green eyes and knowing smile didn't help matters, and before he could stop himself, he was laughing aloud. It was as if a great weight had been lifted from him.

Eve joined in, her pale, lightly-speckled human complexion darkening to a newborn pink. She tossed her short red-gold hair back from her eyes.

The very idea of him refusing her was ridiculous. This single moment with her in his arms was the highlight of his miserable existence. He'd walk through fire to hear her laugh for him.

The tap on his shoulder came without warning. "May I?" Miril asked, his voice falsely courteous.

Jearsen's humor fled. All too soon, this magical moment would end, and it would likely end with the princess held to Miril's chest instead of his own.

"It does not please me to," Eve answered crisply. "You are interrupting a private conversation, Miril Li."

"My apologies, Hir," he grumbled.

Jearsen didn't look at his older brother. He knew what he'd see, the same loathing he'd seen for his entire life. Even the air seemed to lighten as Miril took his leave and rejoined his companions in the crowd.

Eve breathed a sigh of relief. "My apologies...uh..."

"None are necessary. My brother needs no prompting nor heeds any social barriers to such behavior. If anyone but he should apologize, it should be my family...for breeding him."

Her delicate brow furrowed, most likely searching out his family tree...or at least the version of it his father promoted, the perfect family, notably one face short in discussion. "Your brother?" she asked, confirming his suspicions.

Jearsen nodded. "Elder by three years."

"Then you are a rare man, a jewel."

His anger burned brightly, but he forced himself not to snap at her. He needed no one's false flattery, no one's pity...and no one's scorn.

"How did you manage all these years without drowning him?" she inquired.

At once, they were both laughing. Mag's Oath, she was good for his soul!

"It was difficult, I must admit," he offered in a conspiratorial tone.

"I imagine it was." Eve's laughter tapered off. "And what is your name, my stalwart lord?"

He fell into her play. "Jearsen, Hir."

"Jearsen. A fine name for a gentleman."

She brushed against him, causing a most ungentlemanly response. She shifted against him a second time, then backed off a step, as the music ended. Had an entire song passed so quickly?

Eve hesitated, apparently uncertain.

"Thank you again for favoring me with a dance," Jearsen managed, his heart aching that his one chance at such a moment had passed in such a rush.

"Would you..." Her eyes asked favors silently.

"Yes?" If it meant this happy memory would last a little longer, he'd agree to almost anything.

"I would like to take some air. Would you escort me?"

"Yes. Of course."

The crowd parted for them, not that the king's guards would allow men to press in on her. Jearsen held his back straight and his chin up, swallowing chuckles at the shock on most of the noble faces. This was a sight none of his brother's friends would have wagered on, Eve Hir remaining on Jearsen's arm for longer than a body-length...or even that he would garner the courage to ask for a dance, in the first place.

Miril caught his eye for a heartbeat, a sour look twisting his handsome features. Jearsen managed not to wince at that; there would be tension over this, from both Miril and their father.

Eve Hir pressed to his arm as she rounded someone in her path, and Jearsen's heart stuttered at the feel of soft breast through his sleeve. No matter their reactions, it would be worth it. Eve was worth whatever imagined slight he was censured for later.

The crisp, evening air enveloped them, and he stopped, pulling off his jacket and offering it to Eve automatically. Her blush deepened to a stunning crimson, and she took it, drawing it on then cuffing the sleeves to accommodate her shorter arms. Eve took his offered arm again.

"My thanks, Jearsen. It was a thoughtful thing to do."

He smiled, pleased that he'd made her happy. "It was a common courtesy that any man walking a lady into a chill wind should have offered."

"And yet, many would not have offered," she noted.

"Then they are fools who take a lady for granted."

"Yes. I believe they are." She hesitated. "Are you warm enough? I could send one of my guards for a cloak and return your jacket."

Jearsen glanced back, only then realizing that two royal guards trailed three body-length behind them. "No. I am warm enough."

He was, but he would have refused if he wasn't. The guards had been assigned for Eve's safety and propriety. Jearsen would not risk either. He glanced back again, nodding to the guards in thanks.

Eve followed his line of sight, a low groan leaving her lips. "My apologies, Jearsen. My father insists—"

"Not at all. After your sister...and your cousin, for that matter, I would balk to see less care for your safety." With two outright attacks in the first two re-bred women to take mates, if Eve was ever unprotected, someone wasn't thinking clearly.

"Are you a danger to me?" she asked pointedly.

"No. Neither am I Colonel Tirin. I am not armed and am not proficient were I armed."

She squeezed his arm, offering him a wide smile. "Again, you think of me." Eve bit at her lower lip.

"What is it?" Jearsen asked, irked at anything that could steal the light of her smile from him.

"Would you like to sit?" she offered.

Her tone confused him. "If you wish to."

"I meant..." Her face went red as cooling magma. "Oh, I mean no offense."

Her meaning was all too clear. "I tire over time, and it does not always respond as I would wish it to, but there is no pain at this moment. I should like to walk, until you wish not to."

Her smile returned. "Thank you."

"For walking with you?"

"And for not taking offense to my questioning. I have been told that I don't always show the proper respect for the privacy of others."

"Why should I take offense? You didn't assume me less. You asked my pleasure." Few people had done that in his life.

Her brow furrowed. "But questions can be callous and painful," she ventured.

"And often are," he admitted. *Some people mean them to be such.* "But you... I cannot explain the difference." *Of course, he could.* "You don't ask to be cruel."

"Then you wouldn't be offended, if I did?"

"No." Jearsen was slightly surprised that it was the truth. He typically hated it when attention was focused on his leg. "It was a hard birth, too difficult for my mother."

"I am sorry for your loss." She sounded it, which warmed him.

"The will of the gods, I suppose. Or...just a twist of life. I never knew her, but I have heard she was a gracious lady.

"I came feet first."

"My brother Joseph did, as well," she interrupted him.

"Yes, but you had the finest woman healers on Kegin. My mother was not so lucky. The healer did her best, but we were in a remote location... My leg was twisted beneath me, long enough and in a position to do permanent damage."

Eve remained silent, most likely at a loss for a response that wouldn't sound patronizing.

Jearsen found that silence unbearable. "Doctors were summoned, of course, but when nerves are destroyed, they do not always repair themselves. Even in a growing child, when it's most likely for them to."

She nodded. "Then it was an accident. There was no...genetic base for it."

"I assume not." The truth was, he had no idea.

Eve came to a halt, turning to him, her eyes questioning. "You *are* noble."

Out of the corner of his eye, Jearsen saw the guards stop, keeping a respectful distance and preserving their privacy.

He focused on Eve, trying desperately to follow her jumps of logic. "I am." But, what did that have to do with anything, in particular?

"You've not been tested for genetic viability?"

He shrugged, abruptly uncomfortable. "My father felt it was a waste of resources. After all, my disability alone would make it unlikely that any noblewoman would choose to contract with me."

Her mouth worked as if to speak, but only a squeak emerged.

"H—"

"You accepted that?"

"Should I not?"

Eve sighed in exasperation. "No. Of course, you should not."

He grasped at the shadow of words that evaded him. What she said made no sense. "I... Pardon, Hir—"

"Eve," she corrected him.

"Pardon?" he repeated, hopelessly lost.

"Call me 'Eve,' Jearsen."

"Eve?" Mag's Honor, but she confused him.

"You were saying?" She seemed amused by his confusion.

"For what reason would my genetic viability be important? No noblewoman would contract with me. Surely, you know that's true."

She took his right hand in both of hers, not quite meeting his gaze. "Wouldn't one? I see nothing wrong with you."

Jearsen cleared his throat. No doubt, she was speaking in general terms, in terms of what other noblewomen of her acquaintance might do and not herself. He opened his mouth to speak.

"Jearsen," his father called out. "Lelana is ready to leave."

There was no doubt in his mind that it was Miril who wanted to leave and not their father's second wife. He nodded regardless. "I'll be right along."

He met Eve's eyes, aching to ask what that comment had meant, but his father was close enough to hear any conversation they indulged in now. "My thanks for your company...Eve."

Her smile returned. "I will come for you at midday tomorrow then," she stated, as if they'd discussed it at length.

"Tomorrow?"

"You are free to accompany me, are you not?"

"I... Of course. If you wish...still...to have my company, I would be glad to." Jearsen could almost feel his father's eyes boring into him. He reminded himself to continue the pretense that he knew her game.

Eve released his hand and started to remove his jacket.

He covered her hands, stopping her. The guards didn't move; his father did, taking a step toward them that made Jearsen tense and the guards shift two steps closer.

"You'll chill," he managed in a calm voice. "Keep it...until tomorrow. I have others."

"You always think of me."

Before he quite realized her intent, Eve had risen on tiptoe and brushed her lips over his. She glided away, turning to wiggle her fingers in an irreverent 'farewell.'

Jearsen stood in shock, watching her walk away, noting the slight bows of the guards, as they passed him by, trailing in their charge's wake. His mind replayed the kiss, over and over. His lips tingled; his only clear indicator that he hadn't dreamed it was her taste on his mouth.

"Now, if you please," his father reminded him.

"Yes. Of course." Jearsen turned, sighing inwardly at the look of warning on his father's face.

* * * *

Jole looked up in surprise as Eve fairly skipped onto the dais and plopped down in her usual chair. A smile curved her lips up, and she ran her hands over the plain black jacket she wore, cupping the collar to her face to draw in the scent.

"A good night?" he asked, wondering who the man was.

"Wonderful," she breathed. "Magical."

Jole swallowed a laugh. It was good that she was so obviously in love.

Jenneane was less restrained. She took Eve's hand with a squeal of delight. "Tell me everything. Who is he?"

Eve blushed deeply. "When... If we... Oh, Neane. Is it always so complicated?"

"He's right," she laughed. "He must be. The right one is never easy."

Gibril appeared behind Eve's chair and leaned down to finger the shoulder of the jacket. "By Mag, Eve! You cannot be serious," she complained.

Eve slapped her hand away, seemingly furious. "Go find a schaen," she snapped.

"I believe I will," she drawled.

Eve glanced around at her family nervously.

"Eve?" Jole hinted. "A name, if you please."

She hesitated, her eyes pleading.

"Eve," Susan soothed her. "You know he'll simply question the guards if you don't answer. It's for your protection."

"Jearsen... I mean...Jearsen Li," she corrected herself. Eve looked from face to face, her hands fisted in her lap.

"I don't recognize the name," Jole admitted.

Eve managed a shaky smile. "Vetod Li's younger son," she qualified.

He searched his memories for a younger son, but his recollection failed him. That, in itself, was a bad sign.

"You remember, Uncle," Gibril offered. "The cripple."

Eve stood, stalking to her cousin as if she meant to do her harm. "I believe I'll turn in. *Something* has given me a splitting headache."

"Do you need my aid?" Berel asked, rising from her chair at Joseph's side.

Eve met her eyes in surprise. "Yes. That would be splendid." She retreated without waiting for an answer, her guards on her heels and Berel close behind, the latter woman's guards falling into place in the procession.

Jole suspected there would be more of conversation and less of lizor tea in the aid Berel offered. If only he could promise himself it wasn't about to get worse, he might be able to relax into the rest of the celebration.

"Jole, what is it?" his bride asked.

He took Susan's hand, his heart aching. He'd promised himself that all he wanted was his children's happiness, but could he let Eve contract with a genetically unsuitable man?

"Jole?" she prompted him.

"Call for Panor," he ordered the guard at Jenneane's back. He turned to Susan.

"You're going to have Panor report on this man," she accused. "Aren't you?"

He hesitated, knowing she wouldn't like the truth. "For Eve's protection," he assured her. Since Jearsen wasn't one of the hopefuls who'd circled the re-breds before, it was a matter of safety.

Susan pulled her hand away, standing. "I believe I'll check on Eve," she offered coolly. She headed to the stairs, the same litany of guards at her moving back taking their places.

"Excuse me," Jenneane grumbled, already in motion. "I should join Tirin and the children. I believe I could use a lizor tea tonight."

Jole grimaced at the cold reception the women of the family were dealing him.

Joseph leaned toward him, balancing a sleepy Joey on his lap. "If Rebecca was here, it would be unanimous, you know."

"Yes. I know."

Chapter Fourteen

Endl 7, Ri 25-3017

Jearsen straightened his jacket. It wasn't his best jacket. He'd left that one with Eve the night before.

A tingle ran down his spine at the memory of her asking him to use her given name.

It doesn't mean anything of importance, he chided himself. Eve Hir was friendly, unassuming. She simply disliked titles. Surely, it was nothing more than that.

Eve.

He suppressed the need to shiver outwardly. If his father or Miril saw it, they'd insist he was ill, and that would ruin any chance he had of meeting with Eve.

Her transport pulled up, and a guard exited the front seat to open the rear door for him. Jearsen took his time, carefully working his way down the front stairs. He could use the ramp, but he wouldn't resort to that, on a normal day, unless he was injured or his leg was weakening.

This is not a normal day. Eve was waiting for him, and he would approach her as a capable man.

"Good day, Jearsen Li," the soldier offered.

He tipped his head in response, giddy already, at nothing more than the sight of Eve on the seat. Jearsen didn't look back at the house. He didn't dare to. No doubt Miril was glaring at him from somewhere inside.

Let him glare. This is my moment.

The fact that Jearsen had no clue what Eve's plan consisted of was of no consequence. She was here. He would be away from his home for at least a short period of time...with her. It could be Len's Dungeons, and it would be Mag's Paradise, if he was with Eve.

He settled on the seat beside her, and the guard closed them in, taking his place in the front.

There was a moment of comfortable silence, during which he and Eve smiled at each other.

"Are you well today?" he inquired.

"Very." There was something enticing in her tone. Eve patted the folded jacket between them. "My thanks again...for the loan."

"It was my honor."

Her cheeks darkened a few notches, and her lashes lowered.

Jearsen had a hard time finding his voice. "If you don't mind my asking...Eve..."

"Yes, Jearsen?"

He shook his head. Surely she wasn't showing interest in him.

"Jearsen?" she prompted him.

"Where...are we going?" Though it didn't matter, he found he wanted to know.

"Oh..." Her brow furrowed. "I thought that would have been obvious from our discussion last night."

Jearsen re-ran the conversation, but whatever clue was there, it escaped him. "I'm sorry. I'm afraid I don't understand."

She rolled her eyes, but far from making him fear her displeasure, it put Jearsen at ease. Everything Eve did put him at ease.

Her hand slid over the jacket and onto his, squeezing lightly. "We're going to the clinic to have you tested for genetic viability."

Words stuck in his throat. His father had always said it was a waste of resources. Why would Eve want this?

"You will, won't you?" There was a hopeful note in her voice.

I shouldn't accept what I've been told. Eve expects me to challenge the perceptions people have of me. "Yes. Yes, I will."

Even if the tests revealed him a broken man, they would take well over an hour to perform. If his genetics were shattered, he'd emerge no more broken than he'd ever believed himself...but having experienced one perfect day in the company of a young goddess.

* * * *

Eve took Jearsen's hand, trying not to show her attack of nerves. Maybe she'd been wrong to push him into this. What would she do if his genetics were shattered? How could she live with ruining his tenuous hold on respectability?

As if he understood her upset, he rubbed his thumb over her knuckles. After a moment of that calming touch, he spoke. "I must know, Eve. You were right. I cannot accept not knowing."

She nodded, at a loss for words that might comfort him. Realization that he didn't appear to need calming scattered her thoughts. How could Jearsen be so collected, when she felt she might fall to pieces?

The door opened, and the administrator entered, scanning a single sheet of paper. He sat, not addressing them, not even favoring them with an expression Eve might attempt to dissect.

"The determination, Administrator Kevik?" Jearsen asked.

The old man looked up with a tight smile that could mean too many things. "My apologies," he sighed. "I simply cannot understand how this could happen."

"This?" Eve prompted him, forcing her lungs to function so that her voice might sound normal...or nearly so.

His gaze settled on Jearsen, assessing. "How is it that you have never come to the clinic to be trained?"

Eve held her breath, hardly daring to pray she'd understood his inference.

Jearsen shook his head, clearing his throat. "Tr-trained? Administrator... In what should I have trained?"

Kevik placed the paper on the desk and pushed it to Jearsen. The young lord took it with a tremor, a sure sign that he wasn't as calm as he appeared.

The administrator started explaining before it left the desktop. "Jearsen Li, your twenty-fifth and thirtieth gene clusters are active."

Jearsen stared at the sheet, laughing nervously. "And the forty-third and fourth...sixty-second...all intact... Gods...Fion!"

Eve laughed aloud, tears pooling in her eyes in thanks that she'd been right.

He showed her the sheet, disbelief and glee warring on his face. "The healing magic, Eve. My gods... The healing..."

She smiled, nodding her understanding when words failed her. She'd suspected he was viable, but even she hadn't expected he'd be blessed with the magic.

"Would you consent to train?" Kevik asked. "Strong stock like yours is rare. It would—"

"Yes."

"Pardon?" the administrator asked.

Jearsen looked up from the paper between them. "Name a time. I am at your service."

Kevik smiled widely. "If you would give me a moment..." He didn't wait for an answer.

Eve marveled at the speed with which the old man moved.

Jearsen turned to her, pointing out a viability rating in the high nineties. All told, he was nearly as viable as a re-bred but of pure Keen stock. "It's unbelievable."

"Not at all," she assured him.

His smile widened, and he leaned toward her, laying a kiss on her lips softly. Eve gasped for breath, stunned by the move and praying she wasn't misinterpreting it.

"I should not have done that," he apologized. "I've wanted to," he hastened to add. "I've wanted to since you kissed me last night."

Eve forced her mind to function, reaching for the paper in his hand. "You'll be wearing healer blue, Jearsen. You can have anything you want now."

He wrapped his hands around the back of her neck, bringing his lips to within a finger-width of hers. "Can I?"

"Yes. I think you can."

Her eyes fluttered shut. Jearsen wasn't slow and gentle that time. He claimed her, parting her lips, his fingers tangling in her hair as his tongue explored her fully. Jearsen tasted of Cimmeg and warmed wine. Her body burned, aching for more of him.

Spice and fire...but sweet.

Eve fisted his jacket, visions of Jearsen taking her on the desk as Joseph had reportedly taken Berel taunting her.

A clearing throat was Eve's first indication that they weren't alone.

Jearsen ended the kiss, pressing his forehead to hers. "My apologies, Administrator," he offered, though Eve sincerely doubted that he was sorry for kissing her.

"Unnecessary. Would each Trast be agreeable to you? Or...perhaps Ren would be more to your convenience?"

Jearsen placed a quick kiss on Eve's cheek and turned away. "I will invest as much time as is needed. If you feel two days each week would be better than one—"

"Done," Kevik decided. "Trast and Ren each week." He glanced at the file on his desk. "I will send a driver—"

"That won't be necessary," Eve replied.

Jearsen shot her a questioning look.

"I thought... If you would rather have a clinic guard—"

"No." He took her hand, kissing her knuckles. "Not at all."

Eve's heart skipped at that. The taste of Cimmeg echoed in her mouth. Gibby had said that men should be spice and heat. Though Eve hardly trusted her cousin's choices in men, perhaps Gibril had given her the key she needed. Sweet was not enough. Fire and spice were not enough. Perhaps the combination was what she really needed.

Fion's Mercy! If Jearsen is sets me on fire when we're not between the sheets, what will happen when we are?

* * * *

Jearsen strode through the door, staring at the test results for the thousandth time, certain it was a dream he'd wake from soon. He shivered in the memory of the kisses he'd shared with Eve in the back of her transport. If that was a dream, he hoped never to wake.

"The knowledge-seeker returns," Miril drawled.

Jearsen sent him a half-hearted wave. Not even his brother's poking could ruin his mood today.

"Father wishes to see you." He turned toward the offices, adopting a self-satisfied swagger. "Hope you haven't made plans," he sighed.

He closed his eyes and counted a calming ten before he followed Miril to their father's office. Jearsen nodded and sank to the padded chair that was waiting for him. *As if I am incapable of sitting in a wooden one.*

"Jearsen," his father rumbled.

"Father," he replied, schooling his emotions.

"Lelana and I have been talking."

Always a bad sign. Whenever his Father wanted to make an unpopular decree, he said something was Lelana's idea. In truth, Jearsen wasn't certain Lelana had any opinions about him. She was more than a little self-centered.

"You're looking peaked, Jearsen. Perhaps a holiday at the seaside would be an asset to your continued health."

His jaw tightened, and Jearsen swallowed a scream of rage. They were doing this because Eve had shown an interest in him, no doubt. He noted Miril's smirk out of the corner of his eye, fisting his hand in response.

The paper crumpling against his palm reminded Jearsen that he was no longer at the whims of his family. *I'm a healer. I can have whatever I want. I don't want to leave here. I want to know if more can come of my relationship with Eve.*

"Well, Jearsen," Miril stated. "Shouldn't you thank Father for his concern and care?"

Jearsen stood, straightening his jacket. "I'm sorry to concern you, Father, but I won't be going to the seaside."

Silence fell thick around them. His father gaped at him, and Miril's eyes went wide.

"You see, I have a prior commitment to attend to."

"But your health," his father huffed.

Jearsen tossed the paper on the desktop, straightening his spine. "According to this, I am healthier than you are, Father. Since I will be working two days a week at the clinic, I dare say the doctors will be monitoring my health carefully."

"Working?" Miril's voice had an edge of taunt to it, as if the idea of Jearsen working was inconceivable.

"Working," he repeated, meeting his brother's eyes fully. "You see, I possess the healing magic, and one with the magic is bound to serve. You wouldn't want me to default on my sacred pact with the gods."

When neither answered, Jearsen headed to his rooms, smiling at the fact that he'd won himself at least a few days of reprieve. It would take them that long to recover from such a shock.

* * * *

Eve spun in a circle in the entryway of her parents' summer home, noting the half-hidden smiles on her guards' faces when she passed them by. Their opinions of her actions didn't matter to her. Everything was right with the world.

Jearsen was not only viable, he was some of the strongest stock around. That meant he had a purpose, a renewed sense of self...or perhaps a corrected sense of self, which excited him and her by extension.

Better, he was interested. More than interested, if the heated kisses they'd shared were any indication. Eve didn't doubt that Jearsen had been well-schooled by schente, and a tremble of excitement pooled in her at the idea of learning from him. Already, her lips were deliciously sensitized. If she had her way, the rest of her would soon know a similar bliss.

"Eve?"

She stilled at the sound of her father's voice, seeking out his face and focusing on it with a head that spun from more than her dance of joy. He seemed pained; that brought out a streak of concern in her.

"Dad? Is something wrong?"

He glanced at her guards, then to his open office door. "We need to talk."

Steely determination and the burn of anger set up neighborly residence in her gut. So, he'd already started running checks and had concerns. That was appalling. "As you wish." The rest of it wasn't going to go as he wished, she was certain.

Eve preceded Jole into his office, settling on the armed chair her mother typically used while he shut them in. It wasn't where she was expected to sit, which would put her father off balance. Since her aim was to make this the least comfortable discussion they ever had, that was her opening play at it.

He opened his mouth as if to question it then stood on the opposite side of his desk, instead. "You met with Jearsen Li today?" he asked simply.

"You know I did." *I'll be meeting with him often.*

Jole's face contorted as if he bit back a full-blown wince.

"I expect you'll get a full report of my actions within an hour or two." She affected what she hoped was just the right note of resignation.

His eyes widened, but he didn't ask the most obvious question. Instead, he crossed his arms over his chest and stared down at her, what was supposed to be a quelling look. Eve pretended to be oblivious to it.

"Eve... I know you are headstrong, and this must seem terribly unfair to you," he began.

"Uncalled for. Unconscionable. Untenable," she corrected calmly.

"Eve..." he tried to soothe her.

"You didn't balk at Tirin."

"He was a royal guard and—"

"You didn't do investigations on Berel."

"We know her. We don't do formal investigations on most of the hopefuls," he reasoned. "But they are active socially, so..."

"You know them," she repeated. "I suppose the fact that I am coming to know Jearsen is of no consequence."

The double meaning wasn't lost on him. Jole searched out her expression, then her clothing for any signs that she'd *known* him in a more carnal sense of the word. At length, he visibly dismissed the possibility. "There are almost no records of him," he stated plainly. "There is a record of birth, of course."

"Jearsen was home taught by some of the finest tutors on Kegin. In fact, some of the elder ones taught Uncle Michael, in his youth. Since he didn't attend any of the central schools, even those frequented by nobles in search of alliances, there would be no records of it. Since he's never run afoul of the law, there would be no records of that."

She paused for a moment, waiting for Jole to open his mouth just to interrupt him. "His medical records are less populated than most, since he didn't have the opportunity to injure himself as often as other children do. Of course, there's a new entry in them that might surprise you, given your...bias."

"I am not showing a bias," her father protested. "I simply want to safeguard you the same way you would be safeguarded with any other hopeful."

"From a man who has never run afoul of the law?" she challenged. "A man who has lived so completely in obscurity that you didn't realize he existed, until I pointed him out to you?"

"Lived in obscurity or was hidden away by his family? Eve, what if there was a reason he was hidden away? What if he cannot be as full a husband as you wish him to be?"

He didn't state the obvious concern, leaving her to reason her way to it. What if Jearsen couldn't produce viable children for her? Was she prepared to give them up for him? Would her father allow her to? He could disallow a contract that hadn't produced children.

"Considering the fact that Jearsen's viability rating is two points lower than your own, I hardly think his ability to be the husband I wish is at issue. Or the husband *you* wish for me, for that matter." Memories of Jearsen's responses made her lips sing with phantom pressure. "In fact, I am fairly certain it would be a...productive match."

Her father's eyes went hard and assessing. "He's never been tested for viability."

"He was today. Administrator Kevik would be delighted to confirm that Jearsen will be training to use his healing every Trast and Ren...and I will be accompanying him." She let the challenge hang between them.

"Accompanying him?"

She nodded.

"Why?"

"Because it's important to Jearsen. And because...I wish to spend time with him."

Her father seemed to consider that for a moment. Finally, he nodded. "Your presence may help him learn."

His capitulation surprised her. "It may?" He was agreeing without a fight?

Jole smiled. "The healing uses positive energies. If he feels for you as you do for him, it is a very powerful positive energy."

Her heart skipped a beat at the idea of being Jearsen's healing source.

CHAPTER FIFTEEN

Endl 10, Ri 25-3017

"We will break for a bit," Koset offered. "Rest here, mi'lord. I'll have food sent to you." The lowborn healer left them with a bow of his head.

Jearsen laid back into the treatment bed, closing his eyes, exhausted. Who knew the magic could be so draining? For the first time, he doubted his ability to learn it.

The warmth at his side announced Eve's approach. She took his hand, stroking at the palm idly. "What do you think of?" she breathed. "When you work at your healing, what do you think of?"

A smile pulled up at his lips. He'd thought of little but her body since the night he'd met her. Gods, but that was only four days earlier. Forcing such thoughts out of his mind while he focused on the healing was difficult but necessary. "The healing, of course. What else should I think of?" he inquired.

"I thought so."

There was a note of something amused in that reply. Before Jearsen could question it, Eve's hand left his and settled high on his inner thigh, stroking at the well of musk through his trousers.

He stiffened...in more ways than one. His cock was heavy and thick, begging for her to move higher. Forcing back the urge to request it aloud was nearly impossible. The fact that he didn't want to stifle it wasn't helping.

He lay there, letting her tease at him, barely breathing. At length, her fingertips trailed up to his sac, making maddening circles that left him gasping for breath.

"Remember this," she whispered. "When you need to heal, keep half your mind on the instruction and the rest—"

A knock at the door had her hand retreating.

"Come in," she called calmly.

Jearsen opened his eyes and stared at her, barely noting the Administrator's maid setting the food on the table Eve indicated, uncaring of the fact that Eve's body blocked the maid's view of his painfully erect cock. The moment the door closed, their eyes met.

Eve's hand returned to its sweet torture of him. "Eat, Jearsen."

"I don't understand," he admitted.

"Healing comes from positive energies." She made a concerted effort at the nerve bundle behind his sac that nearly brought him off the bed. "I am...positive this will aid in your learning to heal."

Uncertainty ate at his confidence. "And is that the reason you're doing this?" he gasped out.

"Do my kisses feel less than sincere?" she countered.

"No." Her kisses were maddeningly intense.

As if in reminder...or reward, her hand left his sac and her mouth came down on his. Jearsen groaned into her mouth. As always, her responses scorched at his nerves, goading him on.

He tore his mouth away, gasping for breaths. "It is the wrong time and place for this." Gods, if the right time and place emerged, he would have a hard time stopping himself.

Eve licked her lips as if savoring his taste. She lifted a meat stick from the tray and brought it to his lips. "Eat. Then learn your healing."

"And then?" Jearsen prodded, certain there was more.

Her smile was somewhat lopsided. "My transport has privacy curtains."

His cock opined that such a situation would be 'right enough.' His head disagreed. Unwilling to discourage her completely, Jearsen took a bite of the meat and considered it while he chewed.

He swallowed the food then bypassed the remaining meat to lay a kiss on her wrist. "Our first time won't be there, but there are more than a few uses I could put those curtains to."

Eve's eyes widened, and she gasped. Her nod was quick and enthusiastic, and her face darkened.

"Then perhaps I should eat."

"To keep your strength up?" she managed shakily.

Jearsen drew her empty hand to his cock. "I think you'll manage that on your own."

She stared at the ridge extending past her fingers, jerking away at another knock. Her head swung toward the closed door, and Jearsen lifted the tray into his lap to hide his state.

"Come in," he called out.

Eve turned back, her gaze snapping to the tray. Jearsen tipped another meat stick to her in toast and started to eat.

* * * *

Endl 26, Ri 25-3017

The swish of the drapes closing was all it took to bring Eve's body to life. She wished Jearsen had pressed the button, that he'd start making the first move, but she contented herself with his hungry gaze ranging over her.

There was no question that he wanted her, though these assignations never progressed very far. Eve considered stripping her dress off and making her wishes clear, but she had no doubts Jearsen would balk at the idea of making love in the back of the transport...despite the fact that re-breds were known for it and the guards would likely allow it.

Jearsen hardened. Eve trailed her fingertips over the bulge, her heart hammering at his gasp.

"No."

His hand started at her waist, sliding upward until he cupped her breast. Eve arched into his caress, whispering encouragement, her nipple coming to a point against his palm. Jearsen stroked back and forth, teasing at the nipple, his gaze locked on the interaction, licking his lips as if in consideration of what he wanted next.

"Yes." It came out a gasp.

Eve made a note of the driver turning. Her guards knew her orders for them. As long as it was clear that she and Jearsen were intimately involved, they were to drive back roads and park paths. They wouldn't return Jearsen to his home, until it was evident they had no intentions of more than kissing and conversation.

His hand eased beneath the silin, and an uncharacteristic groan escaped him at the contact. He stroked his fingertips back and forth around her distended nipple, bringing her off the seat in pleasure.

"You want to taste." She kept it a whisper, more than aware that he didn't care for the 'audience' of her guards.

His tongue darted out again in answer.

Eve unclasped the waist of the wrap-around and pulled it open around her body. Jearsen hesitated, his eyes lighting at the sight. It was an Earth design for dresses, one that was considered a re-bred style. Even the more adventurous Keen nobles didn't copy it; the more traditional among them would outcast them for the attempt, no doubt.

Jearsen's head tipped forward, and his hand slid to her back. He paused a moment, letting his breath bathe her breast. Then his mouth was there, suckling hard at her.

Pleasurable pulses started in her thighs and womb and worked their way up her abdomen and chest. Eve grasped handfuls of his hair, her breathing coming in sharp gasps, arching further into his hungry mouth. Little flicks of his tongue played counterpoint to the near-brutal sucking motions, and the musk started flowing freely.

He moved to the other breast, more ravenous. The pleasure bordered on pain. Pinpoints and starbursts of sensation drew a series of sharp little sounds from her. Eve bit at her lower lip, trying to remain quiet. There was no way to keep silence when he touched her, but a minimum of noise was called for.

Jearsen didn't like her guards listening to their play. If she slipped, and her noises spiked, it would prompt him to stop for the day. There was nothing she wanted less than an end to this.

As if he agreed, Jearsen eased Eve to the seat, his mouth trailing from one breast to the other. He held himself over her, not quite allowing his weight to settle fully on her. He bathed her with his tongue, sampling her musk, making exploratory ventures down her chest to the meat of her belly.

Eve pushed her hips up, urging him down her body. Jearsen nipped at her lowest rib then started working his way back up. He paused at her breasts, a smile curving up at his lips.

"What?" she managed.

He trailed the tip of his tongue over a spot that sent shards of intense sensation through her. "Can't have that," he murmured.

"Can't—"

Eve arched up at the scorch of ice along her nerves. He was using his healing. He couldn't. Jearsen didn't know what it would do to her.

And I can't tell him. We are sworn to secrecy.

The fire followed in the wake of ice...then pleasure. Jearsen saved her the trouble of trying to fight back climax by sucking at her.

There was no stopping her reaction, but there was also no way for him to connect it to his healing. Eve screamed, one hand fisting in his hair, the other clawing at his jacket.

His mouth covered hers, muting further sounds. His weight pressed down on her, and Eve shifted her thigh against his cock, silently begging him to continue.

Jearsen parted her lips in a series of deep kisses, tapering off as her muscles relaxed and her rioting mind settled. His weight eased away, and he rose up over her, his gaze trailing over her body like a caress.

Eve tipped her hips up, offering him a taste at the source of her most potent fluids...her climax. If Jearsen imbibed, there was little question that they would finish what they'd started.

He swallowed hard, rapt on what she offered. For a long moment, neither of them spoke...or moved.

"Jearsen." She tried to add just the right note of seduction.

His head swiveled back and forth in a negative arc, his gaze never leaving her. "Not here," he rasped. "Not this way." Jearsen straightened her dress, fumbling at the catch, then working it closed.

Eve didn't move. She stayed on her back, spread for him, offering. Jearsen's fingers trailed lazy lines down her hip, then up her thigh, playing at her slit, under her skirt.

"Jearsen." She begged for him, her entire body vibrating in anticipation of completion.

"Not here," he repeated, seemingly more for himself than for her.

She considered that.

Jearsen wasn't comfortable with the idea of intimacy at his home. He probably saw his brother as a rival, though Eve had no interest in Miril.

Though they played at sex games in her transport, any move to retire to her rooms at the summer home or palace would mean a contract first. Even Tirin had to agree to contract, before her father allowed him to spend the night in Jenneane's rooms.

There was little privacy at the clinic, and her guards would balk at the idea of a common inn. It was something princesses simply didn't do, even if lords and royal officers sometimes did.

We need privacy. We need a place that is neither my home nor his.

The solution came in a flash of realization. They only lacked privacy, because Eve followed the rules set for her. Jenneane connected with Tirin by breaking those rules. What she planned wouldn't be easy, but she'd learned a lot from her more adventurous siblings.

"You have tomorrow free?" she hedged, keeping up their whispered exchanges, so the guards would miss what she said.

Jearsen's gaze panned up to her face, and his fingers retreated. "Yes." There was something soft in that, something she couldn't comprehend.

"Go riding with me."

He hesitated then nodded. "Anything you wish, Eve."

She sent up a silent prayer to Fion that he meant it. "I'll come for you on buck...early... Can you eat an early morning meal?"

"I can. I will."

Eve scrambled to her knees and threw her arms around his shoulders, laying a quick kiss on his cheek. "Wear the riding jacket I gifted you."

He chuckled. "Of course. What else would I wear?"

A vision of him nude, loving her astride, as one of the sacred portraits of Mag and Fion depicted, sent a shiver of awareness through her.

The slowing of the transport announced they were nearing Jearsen's home. Eve hurried to smooth his clothing and her own. She stopped in shock at the sight of him sampling the musk he'd drawn from her body coating his fingertips. Jearsen hummed a note that spoke of carnal intents.

Eve opened her mouth to suggest they return to her home. Jearsen hadn't suggested a contract yet, but she was more than willing to. Her words were lost in his kiss, and she moaned at the mixed flavors of their musk.

The front door opened, and Jearsen retreated, settling on the seat and drawing Eve after him. "Tomorrow," he promised. In a whirlwind, the door opened, and he was gone, striding up the stairs to his home.

"Tomorrow," Eve repeated, excitement bubbling over.

CHAPTER SIXTEEN

Endl 27, Ri 25-3017

"You're making a fool of yourself," Miril argued.

Jearsen didn't answer, instead choosing to pat a hand on his war-buck's neck. It was obvious that Miril really meant that Jearsen had made his brother look bad, that he'd bested Miril in an area outside of academics, and Miril didn't like it.

That was just too bad. Eve and his healing magic had given Jearsen purpose. He wouldn't walk away from either for anything, least of all his spoiled older brother.

"She isn't going to contract with you," he continued. "When you are secure in your healing, she'll choose a worthy husband."

"I *am* worthy," Jearsen replied crisply. "Moreso than you are." He tensed for the coming barrage of anger. Whether it was true or not, stating it so boldly had been a stupid move.

Miril half-ran, half-leapt in front of him, blocking Jearsen's way along the path. To round him, Jearsen would have to step onto uneven ground or turn his back on Miril to mount the buck.

His brother flicked the silver trim on the blue riding jacket Eve had gifted him with. "You think this makes you more worthy than me?" he challenged.

Jearsen didn't reply to that, either. It wasn't his healing that made him worthy. Eve had made that clear to him the night he met her.

"What will you do if danger appears? How will you defend her? You can't." Miril pushed him, nearly sending Jearsen to the ground.

That was one argument he couldn't refute. How many times had he considered it? But Eve had guards, and she would always have guards. "Brutality is not the answer to every encounter." Miril didn't understand compromise or using the mind and planning to prevail.

"Sometimes, force is the *only* way." A cruel smile twisted his lips. "For those willing and able to use it. For those who haven't spent their lives pampered and coddled by women."

Jearsen fought the need to roll his eyes. He rounded Miril, choosing to make a show of walking through grass laden with stones and dips that might cost him his balance. "We will discuss this later." *Or never.*

"We will discuss it now." He matched Jearsen's pace, faltering for a moment, as if his body tried to match the gait as well and had to be reminded not to mimic that far.

"I have a prior engagement."

"It can wait," Miril insisted.

"Never keep a woman waiting, Miril. Above all, never keep a woman you hope to contract with waiting."

The blow came without warning, a solid punch to his abdomen that dropped Jearsen to his knees. He bit back a whimper of pain, his breathing coming in ragged streams of air.

No matter what else he'd done, Miril had rarely struck him, never since they'd been adults. Jearsen thanked Fion for Her mercy that he'd escaped it this long. He hadn't remembered it being this painful.

"How dare you even consider such a thing," Miril growled. "Healing or not, the re-breds contract to symbols of hope. You are not worthy of that image."

I am. Berel was lowborn, and she was worthy. Danellan was disavowed, and she was. But he dared not say it now. Not while Miril was in this rage.

Miril grasped him by the collar, his expression hard. He opened his mouth to speak, then looked up in surprise at thundering hooves and a battle cry.

Eve charged down the hillside, her fiery hair uncovered, leaning forward, riding like a soldier into battle. Miril scrambled back, no doubt believing she meant to ride him down. Jearsen struggled to his feet, waving her off, not entirely certain his brother was wrong.

She drew up between them, reaching a hand down to Jearsen. "Can you get up?" she asked urgently.

He ignored her hand and planted his hands on the buck's rear hump, levering his body up by the strength of his arms alone, as he had since childhood. He threw his leg over and settled behind her, grimacing at the pain lancing through his chest. He nestled his body to hers, crowding Eve in the space the notch afforded them, then placed his hands behind hers on the reins.

Eve glared at Miril, turned her mount, and kicked him up to a run, leaving the startled young lord behind. She rode hard toward her parents' summer home, slowing as Jearsen slumped down, groaning. He grasped at her waist with one hand and pressed the other to his aching muscles.

The buck pivoted right and up, stopping in a lush clearing between their lands. Eve brought her left leg up and sat the forward hump sideways, reaching for the buttons on his jacket.

Jearsen grasped her hand, shaking his head. "I'll be...fine," he gasped out. "Just need...to catch my breath."

She nodded, sliding to the ground. "Will you allow me to check it?" Her voice was controlled, nearly devoid of emotion.

"If you insist."

"I do."

He slipped to the ground, slowing himself with handfuls of the war-buck's long fur, hissing out a breath as he jarred the bruised flesh. Eve grasped his arm, steadying him as he made his way to a Garigol tree and sat, leaning against the rough bark.

She knelt beside him, undoing the buttons on his jacket. Jearsen tried desperately to focus on the reality. This was a clinical analysis of his injury, not a tryst. His body dismissed his mind's caution, the sensory input overpowering common sense. The ties on his tunic came next, and before long, he was bared nearly to the waist and rock hard in the bargain.

Eve's fingers trailed over the bruise lightly, her gaze locked on his abdomen. "Your brother does this often?" she inquired.

There was no anger in her voice, no pity, no emotion of any sort. Jearsen had never had so little clue to what she was thinking.

"No. He hasn't touched me in anger since we were children."

She nodded, her jaw tightening. "He won't dare to again."

He fought for clarity, uncertain what she meant to do. Surely, Eve couldn't intend to have Miril killed. Then again, one word to her guards, and she could have him beaten inst—

"Your guards!" Jearsen looked for them frantically. Why was she alone and unguarded? How had this happened? "Where are your guards?" They'd become such a constant, Jearsen had ceased to notice them, unless he was addressing them directly.

A secretive smile curved her lips. "It does not please me to have guards today."

Jearsen's protest died in his throat, expunged as Eve lowered her head and laid a kiss just below the bruise. She trailed her lips down the line of male curls to the vee of his tunic, her breasts brushing over his thigh.

"You should have guards," he managed.

Eve was a sensual Keen woman seeking intimacy, which meant she wouldn't want an audience for what they were embarking upon. But, she was also a Keen princess, and her protection had to come first.

I can't allow this. "No, Eve. Not here." *By Len, it will be the first safe place we land...but not here, exposed and unprotected.*

"You'd turn me away?" she purred.

Her tongue dipped behind his tunic, making promises that scattered his thinking mind. She rose up over him, straddling his thighs, her chest to his, her eyes heavy in arousal. She'd inhaled a healthy dose of musk, and hers wasn't helping him order his errant mind.

"Only as far as a guarded bed," he growled.

Eve shifted further up his body, her heat making his erection issue demands he knew full well he couldn't indulge in. She kissed him, an undeniable promise of what would happen in that guarded bed...if it didn't happen in the very-inappropriate here and now.

Jearsen cupped his hands on the meat of her buttocks and pulled her tight to his body, fitting the hollow between her thighs to the length of his cock through their clothing. Eve rocked back, licking her lips, her eyes opening slowly. Her hands went to the buttons on her jacket, undoing one after another.

He watched her, struck mute in a combination of hunger and longing. Eve would bare her body to him, offer herself, scream in ecstasy for him. Turning her away the day before had been difficult enough, but they'd had the audience of her guards then. They didn't now.

Fion knew he wanted this, but not here. There had to be a way to convince her to wait.

"Have you had a man?" he asked. She'd indicated that she hadn't. It was the one thing he could refuse to compromise on.

She paused, her jacket halfway undone. "No." Her voice was hesitant. Perhaps, she saw his argument already.

Jearsen stroked his fingertips along her jaw. "At your home, with your woman healer nearby," he promised her. *If your father allows such a thing.* "I will not risk you." And his home had no woman healer in residence. Even if he chose to provoke Miril by taking Eve there, it was no safer for her to experience a first completion at his home than it was here.

Eve tilted her head, sucking his index finger into the heat of her mouth then releasing it with a kiss on the fingertip. "You'll have to contract with me for my father to allow it," she informed him in a conspiratorial tone.

His heart stuttered. "Are we going to contract?" He played his fingertip between her lips. "Or, are you telling me that we won't be finishing today?"

Her eyes closed, and she stroked the tip of her tongue around the first joint of his finger. "I suppose that depends."

"On?"

"Are you ready to sign the contract I'm offering?"

Jearsen threaded his hands through her hair and dragged Eve to him, claiming her mouth, groaning as her hands explored his chest beneath the tunic. She shifted against him, mimicking the motions of driving her body around his length. He pulled away, reminding himself sternly that she was without protection here.

"We will sign the contract within a day," he warned her.

"Within the hour," she countered.

He smiled, releasing her so Eve could stand and head for her buck. Jearsen followed, already aching to consummate the union, the soreness from Miril's blow fading to the background. The smile melted at the sound of hoof beats.

Miril topped the hill on the mount that had been prepared for Jearsen, the buck he'd carelessly left behind. He pulled the beast to a stop, his jaw tightening as he scanned his gaze down Eve's body.

Jearsen stepped between them, acutely aware of how much of her body his brother could see. Eve accepted the shelter of his back, working the buttons on her jacket.

Miril darkened, dropping from his buck with a thump Jearsen would have found bone-jarring. He faced Jearsen, his hand fisting until his knuckles stood out white, as if in serious consideration of committing murder.

Jearsen took a calming breath. "Mount up," he ordered Eve.

Her hand pressed against the back of his shoulder. "Jearsen—"

"Now." She couldn't stay on the ground, not when it was likely Miril was about to do something a sheltered princess should never see.

"You're coming." A touch of panic colored her voice.

He nodded, knowing she wouldn't do as he ordered unless she believed it. Of course, he planned to follow her if Miril didn't prevent it, but the fact that Miril meant to educate him in the use of force was impossible to miss.

Jearsen offered his hand without taking his eyes off Miril. Eve set her foot in and vaulted onto her buck with minimal lift from him.

Miril stomped toward them, cycling his hand open and shut. "Send the princess away," he growled.

Eve grasped at Jearsen's jacket collar. He pried her hand off and took a step away. Even if he jumped up behind Eve now, Miril would have him before he was fully over the top and ready to ride.

"Jearsen," she pleaded.

"You should go, Eve," he replied calmly. Miril wouldn't dare injure her; he wanted Jearsen, but there was too much chance of her being injured accidentally if she stayed. "Go collect your guards." He prayed she'd do it to get her out of harm's way...and to ensure that Miril paid in blood for what was about to happen.

As his brother closed on him, Jearsen fisted his hand. He'd never fought, never been encouraged to fight, but if that's what it took to stop Miril—

"Miril," Eve shouted. "If you do this, my father will hear about it."

He ignored her, seemingly intent on Jearsen to the exclusion of all else. Miril reached for his open jacket, and Jearsen reacted.

His fist crashed into Miril's cheekbone. Jearsen watched, shocked, as his brother landed hard on his back, sending up a shower of dirt. His mind wouldn't process this turn of events. Logically, he knew he should mount up and run before Miril found his feet; that fact didn't make it to his body in time.

Miril launched to his feet and threw himself at Jearsen with a scream of fury. Time seemed to move slowly, and yet Jearsen's body didn't react to the coming threat.

His brother hit him with his full body weight, forcing Jearsen back. His leg folded, and they tumbled, wrestling for superior position.

Jearsen threw Miril off and took to his feet, vaguely noting Eve's shouted commands for them to stop. It was a short-lived reprieve; Miril knocked him back again, this time into a wall of silin fur, a wall that moved abruptly away. They crashed to the ground together.

Eve screamed. Realization came with a shock, and Jearsen shoved Miril away, rolling to his stomach, then pushing to his knees. As he'd feared, their blow had startled Eve's mount.

The buck fought her controls, making sharp turns and dodges designed to unseat her. Eve held on tight, her eyes wild. Jearsen had barely reached his feet when disaster struck.

Her mount reared back. Eve held her seat, digging her knees into the buck's sides and leaning fully into the flowing mane. The buck crashed down, arched his back then reared back again, twisting beneath her.

Eve was thrown free. She screamed, her arms reaching out for a handhold to stop her fall. Jearsen shouted out a protest, lurching toward her. The buck streaking past blocked his view of her.

Then he was at her side, searching out her pulse frantically. It was there. *Thank Mag! Thank Fion!*

Her right wrist was at an odd angle that indicated it wasn't simply broken but rather shattered. Blood matted her hair and spilled onto the ground.

Jearsen dragged off his jacket, pressing it to the flow of blood gently...then harder as he rationalized that he had to use pressure. "Eve? Eve, if you can hear me, respond."

"Oh, gods," Miril gasped. "What have we done?"

He would have liked to bristle at the term 'we,' but Jearsen had to admit he was partly at fault for this. He should have attempted to mount up, despite the fact that it would have failed. He should have tried to talk Miril out of fighting in front of Eve.

"You possess the healing magic," his brother all but shrieked. "Heal her."

"I can't heal this much damage." He couldn't heal her wrist in its present condition, but perhaps the bleeding... "We need help." Jearsen looked around, sending up a prayer of thanks that the mount Miril had taken from him was still there. "You have to bring her father and a proper medical transport."

"Are you mad? He'll kill me for—"

Jearsen glared at him. "*This* was an accident, but if Eve suffers permanent damage because of your procrastination, I will see us both dead for it."

Miril backed off a pace, paling at the threat.

"Go. I'll do what I can."

His brother sprinted for the waiting buck and took off at full stride.

Jearsen peeled the jacket back, wincing at the laceration beneath her hair. If he did this, she'd carry the scar forever. *If I don't, she might die from blood loss.* He closed his eyes and prayed for luck then started healing her.

Closing the wound seemed to take forever. Still, Jearsen continued, until he was shaking in the effort; if there was deeper damage, he would do his best to see it healed as well.

He dragged off his tunic and mopped as much blood as he could from his face and hands, then used it to do the same for her face and hair.

Eve groaned, grimacing.

Jearsen placed a hand on her shoulder. "Don't move. Help will be here soon."

"I...I hurt," she whispered.

"I know. I've done what I can for you. The doctors have to set your arm before it can be healed."

She nodded, then sobbed.

"Don't move," he repeated. Jearsen panned his gaze over the clearing, searching for any medicinal plants that might prove of use. "I see something that might help."

"Don't leave me," she begged.

"A few heartbeats," he promised. Jearsen made his way to the closest tree, searching out the budding Garigol. "Just an early bloom or two," he begged of the gods.

There were a few that had just opened. With any luck, they'd produced enough sap to sedate her. He collected them and hurried back to her side.

Jearsen wasted no time. He tore away the stems one by one and squeezed the sap onto his fingertips. He brought his index finger to her lips.

"Eat this, Eve," he ordered.

She rolled her tongue around his finger then sucked it in. Jearsen reminded himself that this wasn't sexual, trying to talk his renewed erection down.

He replaced the index finger with the middle. "Again," he managed in a rough voice.

Eve cleaned finger after finger, her green eyes going unfocused then closing, her muscles relaxing and her breathing evening and slowing. Jearsen sat beside her, arranging his legs crossed under him. He rubbed a hand over his eyes wearily, startling as Eve's left hand closed on his.

* * * *

Jole watched as the mountskeeper tried to get a line on Luz. It wasn't like the buck to be so skittish. Worse, the animal had been taken out while the keeper was at morning meal. He eyed the bridal warily.

Panor arrived at his side.

Jole didn't look at him. "How many are accounted for?"

"Pyter and Eve are both off the estate. Pyter's transport is missing, but Eve's is being maintenanced. We cannot be certain—"

"Pyter," he decided. "It has to be Pyter." Eve had never ignored the safety measures; she'd never ducked her guards as Jenneane often did. Pyter's middle name might as well be 'Irresponsible.'

"The men are already searching, but we don't know which direction he might have—" He broke off, turning to the sound of a rider approaching at full stride.

Jole waited until the lone rider was nearly upon them before he gave up his examination of the half-crazed war-buck.

Miril Li pulled up beside them, bowing his head and gasping out a request to speak. He wasn't dressed for riding. His trousers were light day-wear, his boots scuffed, his silin tunic torn and dirty...and his face bruised.

Jole could scarcely breathe. "Speak," he managed in an even voice.

"It's Eve Hir. She's been thrown."

"Thrown?" Panor thundered, his hand closing on the hilt of his dagger. "You look like battle gone wrong, and—"

"She was!" His wind-chapped face darkened to crimson, and he focused on the struggling mountskeeper. His voice dropped. "I swear it was an accident. My brother and I... I hit him, and he fell into her buck. His leg is weak, you see, and—"

"How serious is it?" Jole asked, interrupting his rambling.

The young lord struggled for words, finally shaking his head hopelessly. "Jearsen said we'll need a medical transport...a *proper* medical transport...and you...your healing magic."

Jole had no doubts he was trying to repeat every word faithfully for fear of missing something of importance.

"He said..." He swallowed hard. "He said his healing isn't enough, but he will do what he can."

"I'll take a tracker from the board. Have them follow it."

Jole didn't give Panor time to protest the need for guards. In the time it took his chief of security to open his mouth to do so, Jole was inside the stable with a bridle in his hand and a tracking beacon tucked in the waistband of his trousers. In moments, he was mounted and following Miril over the hillside at full stride while Panor ran the opposite direction, shouting orders to soldiers he passed.

They were nearly a quarter of the way to Miril's estate before he veered up and off the trail.

Gods, but we might have missed her entirely.

He dropped to his feet beside them, his heart thudding behind his ribs. His mind refused to accept what he was seeing as reality; surely this was a nightmare, and he was asleep next to Susan, all of his children safe in their beds.

"Her arm is shattered," Jearsen breathed. "I gave her Garigol sap for the pain, but I can't heal it like this."

Jole winced at the angle of her hand. It was a good thing Jearsen hadn't tried to heal it. There was still hope to do it right.

"I've healed as much of the head injury as I can," he continued. "I...don't know what other injuries she might have. I don't have enough equipment to be sure."

Jearsen was stripped to the waist, having sacrificed his jacket and tunic to her care. Like his brother, he was bruised and dirty. Unlike Miril, he was dressed for riding, pale, shaking, red-eyed...obviously exhausted and distraught.

Jole lowered himself to his knees, at a loss to do more than check her pulse. He peeled the silin away from her hair, cursing aloud at the amount of blood she'd lost before Jearsen stopped the flow.

"She'll be scarred, I know," Jearsen offered sadly.

"Why did she do this?" What possible reason could Eve have to risk herself this way?

Jearsen closed his eyes as if he was pained by the question.

"Why?" Jole repeated.

"She asked me... We agreed to contract. We were on our way to your summer home. When I realized she had no guards, I insisted we return immediately for them, but...we never had the...the chance to..."

Jole nodded, touching Eve's face gently, all too aware of the risk of jarring her injuries. He scanned her body slowly, looking for other signs, for any pressing situation that he should deal with. His gaze stopped at Eve's uninjured hand.

Even in unconsciousness, she held to Jearsen...her chosen mate.

"I'm sorry," Miril mumbled. "I didn't mean—"

"Wait at the path," Jole barked. "Bring the medical team when they arrive. Tell them we'll need splints and a strap board."

"As you wish, Ri." He retreated.

Silence fell in his wake. Jole searched for the right words to comfort Jearsen, to reassure him, wondering at his need to do so when they both stood at the precipice of losing someone precious to them.

I know this misery. When Susan was taken, when I learned she'd been thrown from Chidan, I felt this. "It's not your fault," he managed.

Jearsen sighed. "I should have talked to Miril instead of striking him. When he came at me, I just....reacted. Eve...Eve always says I think of her first, but I don't think I did this time."

"Didn't you?" It would surprise Jole to find he hadn't.

The young lord's brow furrowed, probably in the mental replay of the events.

"Jearsen?"

"I tried. I got her mounted in the thought she'd be safer on the buck than off. I shielded her with my body. I thought..."

"Yes? What did you think?" Jole prompted.

"I thought the odds of Miril dragging me off her mount and spooking the buck in the bargain were too high to chance. I tried to send her away." A sad smile softened the line of his lips. "I should have known she wouldn't leave me."

"Then you thought of her first."

CHAPTER SEVENTEEN

Endl 30, Ri 25-3017

Jearsen looked at the files in sick disbelief. He wouldn't accept this. He couldn't. The thousands of pages of human medical texts he'd read poured through his mind. Perhaps their methods would work on Eve.

"Are you listening?" Kevik asked.

"I would like to try something," he replied.

Her parents looked up in surprise.

"There is nerve damage," Queen Susan reminded him. "You yourself know—"

"I *know* that Eve challenged me not to accept what I'd been told, and that challenge gave me the power to save her life. I know there was no one with the healing magic except the royal family within four days' travel of me when I had need, and no one thought to ask the royal family to aid me. But I am here...now, when Eve has need of me, by the kindness and mercy of Fion Herself. I know there are human procedures I might be able to bend to our needs. I know, with all due respect to Rihem, that I will not simply accept now that Eve depends on me to challenge myself and the beliefs of the Keen medical community to find something better for her."

She seemed shocked to silence, and Kevik was shaking his head, trying desperately to warn Jearsen off.

"My apologies," he grumbled. "I have overstepped my—"

"No. What human procedures?" she asked urgently.

Jearsen took a calming breath, weak in the relief that he hadn't alienated Eve's mother with his outburst. "The humans use..." He searched for a Keen word and found none to translate to, just as the text had contained the English word. "*therapy...*" He'd had to ask Eve to pronounce it for him, at the time. "coupled with surgery, by which they route past damaged nerve cells or bind broken links chemically."

"The Keen doctors haven't been able to recreate the technique," the queen noted sadly. "The Keen and re-bred Keen physiology is too different."

"What if we don't have to?"

Her mouth worked as if to question him, but nothing emerged.

Jearsen searched for the perfect words to convince them. "I propose a concentrated effort of healing and human therapy...daily...twice daily or more, if she can tolerate so much. By forcing her to use her hand, enticing blood to flow more freely, and concentrating healing along the damaged pathways, I may be able to restore nervous function...I believe."

Kevik cleared his throat. "What you propose is unlike anything we've ever done. Long-term care of this sort is—"

"The humans have done this for almost a century. Are we less dedicated than they are?"

No one replied.

"I am not asking for a team of healers. I intend to take on her care myself." He met Jole Ri's startling green eyes. "With your permission, of course." Until now, he'd been dealing with the Earth-born queen, but this was something any man of his worth would address to Eve's father.

He seemed to consider that. "You have it, but it's Eve's permission you'll need. How do you intend to convince her?"

"However I have to," he vowed. She'd pushed Jearsen to challenge himself; it was his turn to do the same.

The corner of the king's mouth quirked up in the shadow of a smile. "In that case, there is something I should tell you about human genetics...about human re-breds, in particular."

"I've read the files." Since choosing re-bred medicine as his specialty, Jearsen had been voracious in his appetite for both the texts on dealing with re-breds and the human texts. Since re-breds were starting to display throwback traits to their human ancestry, he'd thought it wise to do so.

The queen darkened. "This isn't in the files. It...could give the wrong person an advantage."

The king smiled widely. "In this situation, it could give the right man the advantage in convincing a headstrong but heartbroken young princess."

Jearsen fumbled for speech. "What is it?"

"Eve will find your healing very..."

"Arousing," his mate inserted. "The more intensive your healing, the more pressing her need will be. It's possible to force her to a mating frenzy with the healing alone."

Jearsen worked at what they were telling him. "But, when she was injured..." He'd never performed such an intensive healing, and there hadn't been even a hint of musk from her. It had to be in error.

The king laughed but harshly. "She was unconscious."

"Or drugged," the queen added. "And certainly always in agony. I doubt any aphrodisiac on the planet would have aroused her then."

Jearsen considered that. In the transport, he'd healed her, and she'd climaxed for him just afterward. Could it have been in response to the healing? "What, precisely, are you suggesting, Ri?" he asked carefully.

The king and queen shared a long look before the former spoke again. "You do intend to contract with Eve, as you agreed?" he hinted.

"Whether I heal her or not...if she'll have me and you'll grant your blessing."

"Then, I suggest you use this knowledge to your best advantage...with our full blessings."

Jearsen forced his breathing to even. "I will need a woman healer for our first session," he ventured, half-expecting their shock or anger at his presumption.

Susan nodded. "Syl is available now...or as soon as you need her. If things do not progress as you expect them to today, call for Syl or Berel until...until their presence is not longer required."

"My thanks," he managed thickly. Gods, just the thought that he could pursue her had him ready to.

* * * *

Eve didn't bother to answer the knock on her door. The servants would tend to her, whether she asked them to or ordered them away. Her family wouldn't respect her solitude any more than the servants would, at their direction not to.

As she'd expected, the door opened and someone stepped into the semi-darkness of her rooms.

She blinked her eyes as the lights came up fully, turning toward the door, preparing to shout out whatever intruder dared... "Jearsen," she breathed.

He nodded, but he didn't answer.

Eve straightened her robe with her left hand, burrowing the other beneath the quilts.

Jearsen strode toward her, pulling the blankets back and cradling her hand up. She bit back tears at the disconcerting non-sensation of his touch.

"You will not hide from me," he stated. He pressed his lips to her palm hard enough for her to feel a whisper of touch. "And you will not give up and accept this."

"What choice have I?" Her voice cracked, raw from the crying she indulged in, night and day, whenever she considered what she'd lost.

He turned her hand palm down, sinking to the edge of the mattress. Eve watched, spellbound, as he sucked her index finger into the heat of his mouth. Tears pooled in her eyes. It was unfair to let him hope.

"I wish I could feel it, but I—"

The shock of ice racing up her arm silenced Eve. Heat followed, and she gasped out a breath. The pulse of pleasure that followed was sinfully sweet. Eve's head rocked back and her eyes closed on a moan of delight.

"You feel that," Jearsen taunted.

She started to deny that she'd felt anything in her hand, but she did feel something. It was more than a tingling, less than a burning, a slight sizzle of something unnamable.

Before Eve could question it, the cold came again. Snapping her eyes open, she locked on the vision of Jearsen sucking at her middle finger. The heat scorched along the path, and she cried out in surprise. What was he doing to her? That thought came numbly, as the pleasure made thinking more difficult.

Jearsen tilted his head to one side, watching her reaction. The pleasure traveled her body, making the familiar ache for him reignite. He inhaled deeply, his eyes going hot in the promise of more.

His mouth closed on her ring finger. Eve shook her head, her rioting mind demanding she stop him even as her body begged for more. Jearsen used his healing magic again, his eyes challenging her.

Eve bit her lower lip, panting through the overwhelming sensations, certain he meant to drive her mad. But, how could he know what he did to her? It was protected knowledge. She cried out, half in protest and half in longing, as he took her pinky finger in.

He smiled around it then used his magic. His lips trailed to her palm, and he used it again...the scar at her wrist...the pulse point at her wrist...in quick succession. The bolts of cold, hot, and pleasure overlapped, warring in her system.

Then Jearsen had her pressed to him, his mouth fevered against hers. "Tell me you want this," he whispered.

"Fion, yes, but—"

The next two words were muffled in his mouth. Eve abandoned the rest of her statement, putting her tongue to use against his.

He pulled away, his fingers working the ties on his tunic, then dragging it off. His boots and trousers went next.

She stared at him, hardly able to comprehend that he really intended to do this...or that he still wanted to. Oh, but his pulsing erection attested to the fact that he wanted to.

Jearsen untied the knot on her robe and pushed it away, lowering his head to take one rigid nipple in his mouth. Eve arched against him, begging silently for more. And yet...

"Jearsen, my father—"

"Shhh... Not now."

"But he'll—"

He straightened, shooting her a look that spoke of amusement. "Do you honestly think he doesn't know?"

"Knowing is not the issue. He has—"

Jearsen sealed his mouth to hers long enough to silence her, then broke away. "They sent Syl. She's outside the door."

Eve shook her head, mute in disbelief.

"Very well." He pulled her robe closed and knotted it. "Look for yourself."

She hesitated, and he motioned to the door. Eve rose and ambled toward it in a daze, certain he was joking...praying he wasn't. Her hand shook against the knob, and she glanced back at Jearsen before she turned it.

Syl looked up from her chair, obviously assessing Eve. "Do you need me?" she offered the taking of Eve's barrier for her tactfully.

Eve stuttered out a whispered 'no,' feeling foolish.

"Would you like a lizor tea? Or perhaps lovers' repast?"

Her cheeks heated, and she nodded.

Syl stood and kissed her cheek as she had when Eve was a child. "I had the cooks preparing, in the anticipation of your need. It will only be a few moments." She hurried down the corridor.

Eve closed the door slowly, turning to Jearsen, her heart pounding.

He had settled on the bed, his long legs stretched out and his back to the headboard, still gloriously nude, more scrumptious than Gelgrin. "Tell me you want this," he repeated.

"You know I do."

Jearsen shook his head. "No. I didn't. It might have been the healing, but I'm glad it's not."

"My parents really gave their blessing," she mused. On some level it didn't surprise her.

Anything that would bring her out of her rooms would have looked good to them, she was sure.

He motioned her toward him, waiting until Eve was moving before he spoke again. "Do you still intend to contract with me?"

Eve faltered. "You'd have me...like this?"

Jearsen scowled at her. His hands circled her waist, and he pulled her into his lap, untying the robe and easing it off her body. "I'll have you." His voice was hoarse in some strong emotion. By the other signs, Eve would guess it was arousal. "I'll have you as long as you accept me."

She half-swallowed a scream as he stroked his soft fingertips over her hood. Jearsen drew her face to his, his tongue delving between her lips as his fingers sought out her inner pleasure spot. He played her body expertly, releasing her mouth to watch her.

"Fion," he breathed. "If she doesn't hurry, I'll be inside you before she's returned."

Eve gasped, at the edges of release. Jearsen changed his pattern with a curse, obviously unwilling to let her climax until Syl had returned.

Her senses swam. She turned, straddling his thighs, opening herself fully to his gaze and body.

He groaned, his attention locked on his fingers, sliding in and out through her slit, covered in her fluids. "At the first sound of her approach, I intend to be inside you."

Eve hardly dared breathe, praying for a knock or footsteps in the corridor.

Jearsen's movements became a concentrated effort to drive her over. Eve thrust against him, abandoning silence as her climax loomed. She wanted him inside her too much to care about anything else.

Syl knocked on the door, and Jearsen moved abruptly. His hand retreated, and he pulled Eve toward him, lifting her slightly, then pressing her down as he thrust up into her.

His grunt melded with her cry of pain. Jearsen stilled, his harsh breathing warming her face. His cock pulsed inside her, and she moaned in delight. His length stretched her, making her ache for more.

Eve wriggled against him, smiling as Jearsen groaned. He met her eyes in challenge, rolling his hips to thrust deeper into her.

His cock stretched the band at the face of her os, proving his girth more than the average Keen male, if Syl's instruction was sound...and Eve didn't doubt that. She gasped in the sensation of him retreating and the band contracting again. She'd heard how good it felt when the band was released after full completion. If it felt better than Jearsen sliding free when he was simply erect, she wasn't sure she'd stay conscious past the event.

"That's what you need," he whispered.

Jearsen pushed himself down the silin sheets until he was stretched out flat on the mattress with her astride him. His renewed thrusts played the head through the band at every pass, and Eve rocketed toward release.

"This allows me to reach deeper. You like feeling the stretch of your band."

She nodded, her body pleading for more.

"This is nothing compared to what you'll feel when I swell into the band at completion."

The first whispers of climax teased her. Jearsen groaned in response, his thrusts becoming fiercer. Then she was lost in pleasure, vaguely aware of him praising the sensations of her contracting body...his mouth closing on hers again and again...whispered pleas for her to come back from bliss.

That last brought Eve to conscious thought again, and time moved from a patchwork of images to a steady stream. She started to question why he'd wanted her not to experience the two climaxes overlapping. Eve gasped out the first few words then stopped, savoring the heat of his seed. Jearsen threw his hips up, locking into her band as he swelled. The shocks of her releasing egg sent her over again, and their overlapping sounds were sweet music.

Eve closed her eyes and laid her head to his shoulder, even more exhausted than she'd been when Jearsen barged through the door. His palm settled on the back of her neck, his fingers on her pulse point, no doubt assuring himself she was well.

Her peace was short-lived. "I came here with a purpose, Eve."

She shivered at his no-nonsense tone. Something told her he didn't mean a contract.

"Eve?"

"What purpose?" she asked.

"I intend to help you regain use of your hand...not full use, I'm sure, but whatever we can reclaim."

She raised her head, shaking it to clear the tricks her ears were playing on her. "That's not possible."

"It's never been tried," he corrected her. "I intend to. Your father insists that I need your permission." A smile curved up his lips, and he stroked at the nerve bundle in the base of her spine, drawing her body's attention to the cock still lodged in her band. "I don't intend to take 'no' for an answer."

Forming words was abruptly difficult. "You don't?"

"Absolutely not. There is an added advantage to this plan, though."

His massage of the nerve bundle set her heart pounding, and her legs trembled in another rising climax.

"And that is?" she managed, fisting her good hand in the sheets next to his head.

"It's an intensive program of therapy. That means I'll be living with you, sleeping with you...and..."

He nestled his lips to her throat and applied his healing magic, sending her over into an explosive climax while he lay locked in her stim band. His hand pressed tight to her lower back to keep her from moving and injuring herself in their connected state. She screamed, her throat aching in the effort. Gods, but no one had told her a man could do that.

"Merciful Fion," Jearsen grumbled. "Oh yes. We'll be doing a lot of this."

"Will we?" There was no bite in that, despite his presumption. It was all she could do to force the words out.

"Are you planning on saying I don't have permission to?"

Her bid to answer was cut short by the sensation of his lessening cock releasing her band. It was better than she'd ever imagined it could be.

"Yes." The word was out, before she could censor herself. "I mean...no."

Jearsen raised an eyebrow, waiting for her to construct an answer that made sense.

"Yes, we'll be doing a lot of this. Yes...you have my permission. I won't deny you." Aftershocks racked her at his cock's bucking movement inside her. "Oh gods, I won't deny you anything."

"Then we should have some of the lovers' repast."

Her heart stuttered at what he might mean.

Jearsen shook his head. "To prepare you for the *therapy session.* After that...perhaps."

CHAPTER EIGHTEEN

Wos 1, Ri 25-3017

Jearsen forced his eyes open, trying to decipher what had disturbed him. The bed shifted, and Eve whimpered, trembling in her sleep, her injured hand drawn up to her chest. He reached for her, and she screamed in agony, arching her back.

"It hurts," she sobbed, tears rolling down her face.

Her muscles were knotted, and working at them made her scream again. Jearsen soothed her, rubbing away the tension, using his healing magic on her hand and wrist.

The door slammed open, and the king marched in, his entire body tense and his ceremonial laser-edged sword sheathed but in hand. "What in Len's Unholy Underworld is going on?" he demanded.

At his shoulder, Tirin appeared, looking similarly ready to fight off any attack. Jearsen winced in the knowledge that the guards on the floor below were surely only a moment behind.

"Just a cramp," he replied in the same soothing voice he'd been using for Eve.

"Just?" Jole thundered. "Those screams nearly stopped my heart."

"I'm s-s—" Eve bit back another cry of pain as Jearsen found the bound muscle and started working it loose.

He massaged her wrist, sighing in relief as she relaxed beneath him. "Don't be. There's no reason. This is a good sign."

Jole shot him a look that promised pain, and the arm that supported his sword tightened down, raising it a few degrees. "You call this good? She's in pain."

"She's feeling pain," Jearsen agreed. "But...Jole, she's *feeling*. Keep that in mind."

Eve's eyes opened wide. She stared up at him, seemingly bouncing between hope and misery.

Jearsen managed a weak smile. "This often happens," he apologized. "It is something of a godsend that it took a week for it to. There is pain in regaining use, but I will do all I can to stop it. You have my vow. Typically, the pain recedes as function returns."

"You could have warned me," she grumbled, flexing her hand as she did at the end of their exercises.

"I didn't want to frighten you," he admitted. "Answer me honestly, though. If the work we do can recover even a quarter of your abilities, is it worth this much pain?"

Her father started to protest, but Jearsen motioned him to silence. His heart pounded in anticipation of her answer. The choice had to be Eve's. Jearsen waited patiently while she deliberated what she now knew, praying that Mag would give her the strength to fight.

"Eve?" Jole prompted her.

Fresh tears pooled on her lashes. "If you can recover a tenth... If I live to hold a pen again, even if all I can do is scrawl a likeness of my name, it's worth this much pain and more."

Jearsen brushed his lips over her knuckles, smiling. "You're feeling, Eve. When your hand was all but dead to you, did you dare to hope for so much?"

"No. I didn't."

"Then we work harder. It's working. We have to challenge your muscles and nerves to go further."

She winced, then nodded. "If this progress will be painful, maybe we should retire to the mountain house for the duration."

"No," Jole ordered.

Eve turned to her father, seemingly fighting for a steady stream of air. "Dad?"

Tirin turned and left them, probably to avoid the scene that might be coming.

Jole didn't hesitate. "I've watched you learn to walk and talk, ride and climb. Don't make me miss your first steps...even if you fall."

For a few moments, they stared at each other, Jole stiff and tense, Eve recovering her senses. At last, she extended her injured hand to Jole, flexing it as her father wrapped his hands around it.

"Within a month, I'll hold it," she promised.

She may be able to. Already, she has some movement in her thumb.

Jole nodded, swallowing hard. "I'll hold you to that."

"A princess always keeps her word."

CHAPTER NINETEEN

Wos 25, Ri 25-3017

"Is it too much?" Jearsen asked.

Eve smiled weakly. "Nothing is too much."

It was a stretch of the truth, he was sure. She was exhausted. Every day of work seemed to leave her more drained. She laid her head back on the edge of the tub, fighting off sleep as the hot, churning waters of the bath buffeted her sore muscles, and the fragrant steam rose around them.

His eyes narrowed, and he calculated the strain on her system. "Perhaps we should skip a few—"

"No. You said it yourself. The best results will come of prompt and continuous care."

He shifted his gaze away. "Of course." Jearsen cursed himself for saying it. Now that Eve believed it, she was relentless. "There are still times to rest the muscles and let them heal," he ventured. "Look at what you've accomplished so far. You're starting to gain control of your fingers again."

But not sensation. Ghostly pressure and excruciating pain were the only sensations she'd managed.

"Maybe one session," she conceded.

One per day, for several days. But, he'd argue her agreement to that later. For now, she needed rest.

The subject temporarily closed, Jearsen rubbed out the afternoon's therapy knots. Eve closed her eyes, murmuring her thanks to Berel for the lizor berry tea with the single sand of olum she'd offered.

He flattened her hand against his chest, stretching the muscles out with light pressure. She chuckled, bringing his head up. The sound was unexpected...unusual for this sort of exercise.

"What is it?" he asked.

"Your hair."

His hands went still, and his mind reeled at the implications of what she'd said. "You... Keep your eyes closed."

She raised her head. "Jearsen?"

"Closed," he repeated gruffly. "Just...feel for me." *Fion, please let me be interpreting this correctly.*

Her breathing hitched, but she nodded and eased her head back, giving him leave to experiment.

Jearsen turned her hand palm up, stroking his fingertip through the bowl of her hand. Eve shivered at the sensation, and her muscles tightened, but she didn't draw away.

"Does it hurt?" he asked urgently.

She laughed, a tear escaping her closed eyes. "No. It's wonderful. Who knew a simple touch could feel so good?"

"Good. Keep your eyes closed."

She hummed her agreement, her smile wide.

Jearsen grabbed a bottle of cleansing oil from the tub side. "Tell me what you feel." He poured a little into her hand.

Eve's fingers jerked into a curl then relaxed. She eased her thumb into the puddle of oil. "Tepid. It's not water from the bath."

"It's not," he encouraged her.

Her thumb came up, and she rubbed it against her middle finger. "Slick..." Her brow furrowed. "Cleansing oil?" Her tone said she wasn't certain and was afraid of being wrong.

Jearsen crowed, capturing her lips in a kiss while she washed the oil away in the churning bath. He pulled her hand up again, dipping his face to press his chin to her palm. "Tell me what you feel."

She gasped. "You need a shave."

He laughed heartily at that. "Yes, I do."

Eve raised her hand then moved it to the left, her eyes still closed tight. She traced his lips slowly. "So soft," she whispered. "So warm."

He laid a kiss on her fingertips. "So beautiful," he replied. "Come on. Let's get some practice. I think we can agree to replace one of your therapy sessions daily with sensory retraining?"

She opened her eyes, offering a blatant expression of hunger. "What did you have in mind?"

* * * *

"Dad! You have to see this," Jenneane shouted, her eyes glittering and her color high.

Jole pushed up from his desk, smoothing his tunic as he crossed the office toward her. "What is it?"

185

His eldest daughter grasped his hand. "You just have to see it," she repeated.

He hesitated, noting the tears misting her blue-green eyes. "What is it?" he repeated. Though she was smiling, it was obviously something bittersweet to make her cry. Jenneane didn't cry easily.

She turned away, running for the rear corridors. "You won't believe it."

He followed her, soldiers ducking out of their path, matching her pace halfway down the kitchen corridor. Jenneane stopped short, hanging on the kitchen doorway, her smile radiant and a tear spilling down her cheek. Jole followed her line of sight.

Eve sat at the kitchen work table, blindfolded, her injured hand cupped open in Jearsen's, trembling lightly.

"Are you sure you want to try another?" he asked.

"Yes." Her voice was strong in decision.

Two of the cooks shifted as if in unease, and Househead Vila murmured a prayer to Fion for mercy, her hands fisted in her work jacket, leaving uncharacteristic wrinkles. Jole found he was holding his breath, though he didn't know why he was.

Jearsen reached to the work table with his free hand and plucked a ripe lizor berry from an iced bowl. He raised it, then dropped it into Eve's palm. She recoiled, and he held her hand in place.

"Tell me what you feel," he requested.

"It's cold," she complained.

"Good. And... What else, Eve?"

186

She curled her thumb around the berry. "Firm but..." Her nose curled. "Sticky. Bumps...wedge-sh...shaped. Lizor berry?"

The cooks cheered, and Jole let out his breath in a gasp of surprise, his lungs aching. Jearsen looked around at him, smiling. Jole nodded his thanks, cursing the fact that Susan wasn't here to see this moment.

"Another," Eve begged, dropping the fruit to the table blindly.

"Of course." Jearsen used a wet cloth to clean the juice from her hand, dropped the soiled fabric on the table, then motioned for Jole to remain silent and waved him closer.

One of the cooks laughed into her hand. A glare from Jole and Vila combined silenced her. Eve turned her ear toward the sound.

"No using your other senses," Jearsen chided her.

She darkened, nodding.

Jearsen raised her hand, pressing it to Jole's cheek.

Her forehead furrowed, half-disappearing into the wide blindfold. "Clean-shaven, which means it's not you, this time." Eve reached for his collar, scowling when she encountered no uniform jacket...thus no insignia she might be able to detect.

Jole smiled at her strategy.

Her hand returned to his jaw, paused, then traveled the line to the back of his hair and down to his collar. "Ahh... Too long to be Joseph or Tirin. Too thick to be Pyter's." She hesitated. "I hope this is Dad," she whispered.

"It is," Jole managed in a cracking voice. He drew her hand to his lips and laid a kiss in her palm. "It most certainly is."

Eve threw herself into his arms, laughing.

CHAPTER TWENTY

Fim 1, Ri 25-3017

Jearsen bit back a sigh, reaching for her hand. "It's time to rest."

Eve pulled the pen out of his reach. "No. I'll get it right."

"Your hand is shaking." There was no way she could write her name this way; she could barely hold the pen, and her fingers were twitching in announcement of serious cramps to come.

"I know that," she snapped, grimacing as she pressed the pen to paper.

"Eve, it's only been ten weeks. Give yourself time. The progress you've made—"

"I want to do this," she insisted, her stubborn streak in full swing.

"This is ridiculous." Jearsen snatched the pen from her hand, tossing it away as she collided with him in her bid to retrieve it.

His knee folded, and they crashed to the rug. Eve tried to grab the pen, and Jearsen rolled her the opposite direction, trapping her beneath his body. She struggled but weakly, settling into his stroking hands, her color high.

"Now," Jearsen whispered, brushing his lips over hers. "Why are you so determined to hurt yourself?"

Eve darkened, shifting her gaze away.

He considered that. It wasn't as if she wanted to sketch. Eve had stated repeatedly that she wanted only the most basic control of a pen, and the human-style vid programs Pyter had researched in the Keen database had allowed her to design again. Why would she be so desperate to sign her name?

Realization came like a roll of thunder. Jearsen stroked her cheek. "We can have your father bear witness to your intent. He's been willing to since the first day. I've been willing to accept that."

Eve sobbed, shaking her head. "I'll sign it. I *want* to sign it. It's important to me. Can't you see?"

"I see, but I cannot understand why you're rushing this. The contract will still be there for us tomorrow and next week...next month...next year, if needs be."

Her eyes widened, and she tensed. "No. It has to be soon." There was a thread of desperation woven into her words.

"Eve, you're not making sense. Should I call for Syl and Berel? Or perhaps your—"

Her cheeks went crimson, and she swallowed hard.

"Syl and..." He reached a hand over her good shoulder, massaging knots of muscles.

She arched up with a groan, her eyes closing, her skin heating. Her musk flowed freely, announcing her arousal.

"Merciful Fion," he breathed. "I'd assumed it was the therapy. I didn't realize." It was so easy to miss. Her muscles were knotted naturally from their work to regain use of her hand. They were often in the churning bath or with heating pads wrapped around her to encourage healing; that would make the chill of her pregnancy signs and the heat of her schen nearly impossible to detect. "By Mag's name, I didn't realize."

Memories of their sprawl to the floor and scuffle for the pen assaulted him. She was pregnant. What had he done?

Eve bit her lip, nodding, her breathing quickening.

Jearsen lifted her, depositing Eve to the mattress and settling next to her. "I'll get Berel." After that fall, he had to. He would take no chances with their child together.

Her hand circled his neck, burning hot, massaging his nerve bundle, bringing him to aching readiness.

"I might have hurt you or the babe when—"

She pulled him down, sealing her mouth to his, making her needs known. Her lips caressed his cheek, and she nipped at his ear. "No one was hurt. You could never hurt us. You always think of us first."

His mind barely functioned at that. "Berel should check you."

"After."

That one word was his undoing. How could a single word beg and order, seduce and end discussion firmly?

Jearsen pulled at his trousers, baring himself. He shoved her day dress away, thrusting into her, claiming her with a purpose. Her nails bit into his back through the silin tunic, and she whispered a plea for more. His thrusts came hard and fast, and she screamed his name.

"You are mine, Eve," he informed her. "Whether your pen has touched the contract or not, you are mine."

She nodded frantically, gasping out something that made no sense but sounded of agreement.

"My child rests in your womb, only the first of my children you'll carry."

Her sheath clenched around him, and she moaned.

"The first who dares call our children bastards will die." Jearsen forced back his climax. "Contract or no, they are our children of intent to contract."

Eve climaxed, forcing him over with her.

SECTION THREE:
Kyra

Damaged Goods

CHAPTER TWENTY-ONE

Maiden No More

Fim 16, Ri 25-3007

Kyra peeked from the cabinet Gibril had directed her to, gasping at the sight of her older sister. She shivered, wondering what Gibril meant when she promised Kyra 'an education that was long overdue.' If Gibril's state of undress was any indication, Kyra wasn't sure it was an education she wanted.

The two schaen came into the bedroom, huge men who were easily two head taller than Gibril or Kyra. Predictably, Gibril wasn't intimidated by such specimens. She glided between them, running her fingers over chests that were shaved in the manner Gibril liked.

Kyra bit her lip as the men hardened, their cocks jutting against the silin lounging pants they wore. To Kyra's untrained eye, they were huge. She couldn't imagine what lay beneath the silin fitting in a woman, but Gibril seemed to manage well enough with the schaen who serviced her.

The men knew Gibril's tastes. She didn't have to direct them to pleasure her. The taller one dropped to his knees, suckling at Gibril's breasts, nipping at her nipples. Gibril wound her hands in the man's hair, throwing her head back and issuing sounds of pleasure.

Kyra furrowed her brow, watching the second man in confusion. He retrieved a wooden box from Gibril's bedside table. She moved closer to the gap in the door, trying to see what the man was doing. He removed a long, thin contraption made of ruv.

Gibril cried out, and Kyra momentarily forgot the strange device. The schaen kneeling in front of Gibril had his fingers buried inside her, moving them slowly in and out.

Kyra squeezed her thighs together, looking at her erect nipples in surprise. An ache settled in her womb and wetness wept from her core to her thighs. She took a deep breath to calm her nerves, and a wave of arousal assaulted her. Kyra reeled. *Pheromones*, her mind numbly supplied for her. Their musk was drawing her into their mating frenzy.

The first schaen lowered himself to the floor, trailing kisses and nipping bites down Gibril's body while she spread her legs wide for his attentions. Kyra's eyes darted back to the second schaen. He had lowered himself as well. He leaned Gibril forward slightly, kissing the globes of her ass reverently.

Kyra grimaced as he prodded his tongue in the puckered ring of Gibril's anus. Her attention moved to the first schaen, seeking something more enticing to her own senses. If nothing else, that schaen was a beautiful model of the male form.

That is more like it.

His mouth was pressed to Gibril, moving against the hood of her pleasure. Kyra moved her thighs against each other restlessly. The schaen was relentless: licking, sucking, grazing his teeth over it.

Kyra dipped her fingers through the split in her robe and into the well of her musk, the heel of her hand granting delicious pressure to ease the ache in her hood. *Damn Gibril to Len's Dungeons for this.* Her sister knew that Kyra's arousal would be heightened by the scent of their sex antics.

Gibril jerked, and a strange buzzing caught Kyra's attention. She moved her eyes to the second schaen. Kyra flushed, her breathing harsh in her own ears as the schaen seated the buzzing ruv device deep in Gibril's back orifice.

"Yes," Gibril panted. "That's wonderful."

Kyra stroked herself slowly, swallowing a cry of pleasure. Her breathing hitched as the first schaen licked designs around her sister's hood. It certainly looked wonderful. And the smell was beyond sublime.

As if taking some unspoken cue from Gibril, both schaen rose. The man behind her cupped Gibril's breasts, kissing at her neck and shoulder. His fingers flicked and pinched at Gibril's nipples. Gibril fisted a hand in the schaen's hair, grinding her body into his and wringing a groan from the big man.

The man in front cupped Gibril's face and kissed her, a deep, searing kiss that made Kyra's lips tingle in empathetic response. His fingers played at Gibril's hood. Kyra bit back a groan as her own moisture ran down her thighs.

"Shall we pleasure you now, Hir?" the first schaen asked.

A lazy smile curved Gibril's lips. "I think your brother schaen will be sufficient for this afternoon," she commented in a teasing tone.

A look Kyra would classify as hurt crossed the schaen's face. "Gibril Hir?"

"You've served me well." Gibril ran a fingernail down his chest, licking her lips hungrily.

Kyra licked her lips as well. That schaen would taste wonderful, the musk of his arousal on his skin.

"I thought so," he replied uncertainly.

Gibril leaned toward him, nipping at his chin. "You're one of the finest schaen I've ever had, but you'll have to leave me soon."

He grimaced. "I know."

"I have a special reward for your—" She groaned as the schaen behind her pinched at her nipples again. "Your tireless service."

His eyes glittered. He pressed his body to Gibril's. "I'm sure it will be an excellent treat, Hir."

Gibril pulled his head to hers, biting at his ear and whispering something that made him gasp. The schaen stepped back, his smile wide and his cock pulsing behind the silin.

"Make a good showing," Gibril whispered, "and you will have your reward. Remember what I said."

The schaen made an excellent show. He stripped the lounging pants off, his cock jutting out from his body. He played at his length with a fist wrapped around it.

Kyra glanced to Gibril and startled. Her older sister wasn't watching the impressive show. Gibril and the other schaen were too involved in each other to notice much of anything.

The schaen leaned Gibril forward, covering both her hands on the bed rail with one of his. He dipped his body low to seat his cock in her core, then straightened, lifting her fully off the floor, impaled on his length. The schaen pressed his free hand to her lower abdomen, thrusting into her in fierce motions.

The first schaen stroked his length slowly. Kyra locked on the motion, sure that he had to climax soon.

Tireless. Oh, Fion. Gibril said he was tireless. Does she intend to take this schaen when the other has finished and go to completion twice in a row with no break? Kyra shivered at the thought of it.

Gibril cried out harshly, and the schaen's cry mixed with hers. Kyra didn't spare them a glance, her gaze still locked on the first schaen. Kyra groaned aloud as Gibril cried out again, announcing her release of an egg. The scent of their completion tantalized her senses.

The other schaen moved abruptly, striding to the cabinet and pulling it open, a striking figure of a male. Kyra shrank from him, straightening her robe over her thighs.

The man brought her fingers to his mouth, sucking them in, his tongue hot and thorough, finding the sucre that coated them. Kyra felt that licking all over her body. Her breasts tingled and her core wept more of her fluids. Her legs shook beneath her.

His eyes locked on hers, and his nostrils flared in arousal. "You taste so sweet," the schaen growled. "Did it excite you to watch, little princess?"

Kyra darkened.

"It's a natural thing to be aroused."

He pulled her hand to his cock, encouraging Kyra to fondle him. She groaned, intent on the heated shaft gripped in her hand. Kyra licked her lip, imagining that heat plunging into her. She could have that. She understood now that Gibril's gift to her schaen was giving him to Kyra.

"Are you ready for me?"

Oh, Fion! I am more than ready for this man.

He lifted her from the cabinet without waiting for her answer. She moaned as he cupped her buttocks and pulled her to his cock. His mouth came down on hers. Kyra met him fully, her tongue mating with his as she wanted the rest of him to mate with her.

The schaen opened her robe and lifted Kyra to suckle at her breasts as if she weighed not a thing. The room spun, and the bed was suddenly at her back, the schaen's body delicious weight on her.

"Slowly," Gibril cautioned. "She's untried and intact."

Kyra pulled at him, the fever in her body driving her beyond reason. Untried or not, she wanted him. The schaen kissed her again. Kyra held his mouth to her, seeking his cock.

He guided her hands away and pressed them to the bed next to her head. "Hold her as the woman healer would," he breathed, laying a kiss on her throat.

Gibril took her hands. Some dissenting voice in Kyra argued that there should be a woman healer present for this, for a schaen taking her barrier. The argument was lost in a wash of pleasure as the schaen worked his way down her body.

"Let me help," the other schaen pleaded.

"No," Kyra gasped.

"She's mine," the schaen pleasing her growled.

Kyra bowed up to his mouth as he buried his tongue in her sheath. *His. Yes, I belong to this schaen.*

He possessed her utterly, playing her body expertly until she shattered around his teasing tongue. The schaen rose up over her, seating his cock in her entrance. The other schaen groaned as if he was in pain, and the one over her shot him a scowl.

"See to your mistress, Gibril Hir," he barked. His expression softened as he looked back to Kyra. "Do not touch Kyra Hir."

Kyra nodded, encouraging his possessive attitude. She pushed back slightly on his cock, forcing him a few finger widths further into her and groaning at the sweet feeling of stretching for him.

His hands bit into her waist. "Are you ready for me?" he whispered.

She nodded slowly.

His thrust filled her abruptly, and he captured her cry of pain in his mouth. His hands massaged her body and enticed her to relax around his length. The schaen didn't move for long after her responses were fevered again. Kyra felt as if she could die with his cock deep inside her and his mouth possessing hers.

He pushed back, laying teasing kisses on her lips. "Are you ready?" he asked again, his voice rough and body taut in his restraint.

"Yes." Her voice was a plea. Kyra would give anything to know full completion.

The schaen rocked inside her, pushing her higher, murmuring encouragement to her. Kyra lost herself again, her climax stealing her breath.

He bucked his hips, pressing her hard to the bed. His cry of completion merged with hers, his sterile fluids flooding her body. His cock thickened, locking into the band at the gates of her womb.

Kyra felt her breath catch as the shocks announced her egg releasing. She pulled at Gibril's hands frantically, panic replacing her arousal. She couldn't breathe. The world faded away.

* * * *

"What did you think you were doing?" her father roared.

Gibril's voice was little more than a whisper. "Maiden brides don't have a woman healer present," she protested weakly.

"There is one in shouting distance in case of something like this. There always is. The only reason your precious schaen will be allowed to live is that he saved her life."

Kyra groaned as something shifted within her.

A hand touched her cheek. "Kyra?" It was her father.

She opened her eyes, taking a breath painfully. It felt as if her ribs were fractured. Kyra was empty, lonely. It shouldn't have been like this. Her schaen's arms should have held her in her afterglow. A tear ran down her cheek.

Michael brushed the tear away, his face tortured. "You'll be fine now." He glanced toward the foot of the bed. "Syron?"

Kyra shook her head in confusion. What went wrong? Why was the woman healer here? She jerked as a pain inside seared her.

"A small tear," the woman healer reported. "I imagine he had no choice if he was to save her."

Tear? Save me? Kyra's head spun. She tried to reach out to her father, but her body was leaden and unresponsive.

"Very well," Michael decided. "I will grant his retirement, as he was promised."

Kyra sobbed, squeezing her eyes shut tight. Of course. The schaen took her barrier. By law, she would never see him again. Wherever his continued service was, it would be nowhere near Kyra.

A cup touched her lips. "Kyra, you have to drink this," her father soothed her.

She swallowed a mouthful of the lizor berry tea, thick with a hearty dose of olum, gagging on the bittersweet aftertaste.

"More," he instructed.

Kyra swallowed another mouthful, the olum making her feel warm and relaxed.

"Will there be any lasting damage?" Michael asked quietly, stroking his fingertips over her cheek.

"No," Syron assured him. "Though she won't be able to take a schaen for at least a month, as if she faced the mother's fast."

"Never," Kyra managed in a thick voice. "I'm never touching a man again."

The room went deadly still. Kyra forced her eyes open, locking on the fuzzy image of her father.

He nodded slowly. "If that is your wish, I will support it."

Chapter Twenty-Two

Zor 2, Ri 25-3017

"What did you just say?"

"I want you to be the father of my child." Kyra's voice was calm and seemingly rational, but the words were completely out of character for her.

Steden took a moment to sort through his rioting thoughts. "I thought..."

She'd said it for how many years? She wouldn't have sex again. She did her duty by donating eggs for implantation in genetically-shattered women, entubated and sedated so her condition wouldn't kill her in the process. Now she wanted him to sleep with her? After all these years of wanting her but playing the 'safe, male friend?'

"I plan to be inseminated...the same way they take my eggs. I want a child, Steden. Will you help?"

Now it made sense. His heart ached at what she was asking. Kyra wanted him to stroke off to the loop tape of sex with her he'd secretly concocted in his fevered mind and held to all these years. She wanted him to let her carry and deliver a child he'd fathered, a child she had no intention of sharing with him. It was awful. It was unconscionable.

"I'll do it." If Kyra was never going to take a husband, never going to let another man into her bed, it was the only way she'd ever have a child of her own. If he ever got over her, he might have one with another woman.

She rounded his war-buck and threw herself into his arms, hugging him tight. "Thank you, Steden. You don't know what this means to me."

The same thing it would mean to me, if you agreed to more than insemination to get that child. Gods be praised, if you agreed to contract with me. He smiled and nodded, trying to ignore the press of her lush breasts against him and the weight of his cock behind his trousers.

She started to bounce away, stopping to press a hand to her back. Kyra had always had this problem when they'd ridden for an extended period of time. He moved toward her automatically, releasing his buck to the mountskeeper and motioning the old man away.

"Sit," he urged her, guiding Kyra to the floor and kneeling behind her.

She peeled off her riding jacket, and he did the same. It wasn't until he started kneading her sore muscles that he realized again that she let him touch her so intimately...only Steden. Even her father wasn't welcome to do this.

I wonder... How many years had he thought about exploiting this interaction? He'd never force Kyra to bed with him, but perhaps awakening her to the idea that a man's touch could be pleasant?

Steden rubbed at the lower nerve bundle along her spine, smiling as Kyra groaned in pleasure. She arched her back to urge his hands to where she wanted them most. Her scent bloomed, and her nipples came to points against her silin tunic. That was all he needed to know.

Whether she acknowledged her arousal or not, her body recognized Steden as a man and craved his touch.

He moved one hand to the bundle of nerves at the base of her skull, circling the spot with the same precision that sent his schente into a mating frenzy. It was certain not to have the same effect on Kyra, due to her phobia about intimacy, but it would feel good, and that's what he wanted her to know. Kyra shifted her thighs against each other, an unconscious sign of rising arousal.

The pulse point at her throat was next. Kyra laid her head back, her hair cascading over his shoulder, her eyes closed, her lips slightly parted. Steden longed to taste her lips, but it was too soon for a move like that. He concentrated on her back, working his fingers down her spine to the bundle of nerves he'd started with.

Kyra groaned his name, tipping her head to nestle her face into his throat. Steden smiled at the move. She was taking in their mixed scent, drawing the aphrodisiac into her lungs at the urging of her subconscious mind.

Steden stroked his fingertips up her palms, pausing to circle his thumbs over the pulse points in her wrists. "May I continue?" he whispered.

"Please, Steden." She trembled, shaking her head in jerking motions as his hands stilled in wait of her answer. Kyra turned toward him, her eyes pleading with him.

He nodded, laying Kyra back on the scattered dry redgrass. "Close your eyes."

She complied, placing her trust in him. Steden's heart ached. He'd thought she'd never trust him after that careless schaen.

He stroked at her wrists again, watching her shifting in response, her breasts rising in mute offer, her thighs pressing together as he worked his hands up to the nerves at her inner elbow. Kyra rolled her hips, her body seeking the pleasure her scarred memories denied her.

Steden caressed the sides of her ribcage, running his thumbs down her stomach. Kyra bit her lower lip, bowing up into his hands.

He stroked the damp hottel-weave between her thighs, shivering at Kyra's low cry of pleasure. She was beautiful...so sensual. All that passion wasted on a schaen, then bottled away.

Kyra moved against his hand, riding his fingertips. "Closer," she begged.

Steden bit back a groan of delight as she pulled the buttons on her trouskit open, tipping her hips to push the garment away. He leaned over her, eye-to-eye, as he played at her unclothed body.

Her eyes dilated. She opened her mouth as if to speak but no sound issued forth. Steden sobered. What if Kyra was asking him to stop? What if he'd gone too far? He eased his hand back, aching for her, heartsick that he might add to her trauma.

Kyra shook her head, grasping at his hand. "No. Please."

"What do you want?" Steden asked. He wouldn't proceed without a clear picture of what she thought would happen next.

She raised her head and cocked it to one side, sealing her mouth to his, her tongue sparring with his. Her body pressing against him sent his mind skittering into the dark corners in which he'd seduced her a thousand times in his dreams.

Steden groaned aloud as Kyra opened his trousers in a single tug. She pulled at his length, guiding the head of his cock to her slick channel, her other hand pushing his clothing away.

He broke off the kiss, his mind rioting. He hadn't planned to go this far...only as far as bringing her to simple release. "We shouldn't," he stammered. Though it was unlikely that Kyra would suffer asphyxiation in subsequent encounters, it was safer to have a woman healer close-by for her next few matings.

Tears pooled in Kyra's eyes. She played the head in her fluids, pleading with him silently not to stop. Steden clenched his jaw, trying to find the words to ask her to wait to reach the house. Though her family was there, they were sure to approve as long as a woman healer was standing by; they'd wanted Kyra to resume a healthy sex life nearly since the moment she'd been traumatized.

Here? With the mountskeeper just outside?

He won't bother us. He wouldn't dare.

Kyra bucked her hips, encasing Steden in her tight body. She rolled her hips, pushing him further with each movement. Steden gave in, matching her movements with deep thrusts, increasing speed as she did, until they were in a fever of touching, tasting...driving each other to ecstasy.

She grasped at his waist, her body pulsing rhythmically around him. "Now, Steden," she gasped.

He lodged his cock deep inside her, crying out harshly as he filled her with a draining rush of his seed. His cock thickened and bit into her stim band.

Kyra's breath seemed to catch in her lungs. She looked at Steden, wide-eyed, her hand fisting in his tunic in something resembling panic, a tear spilling down her cheek.

Steden levered himself up, reaching for her chest with one hand, uttering a harsh string of curses. He'd have to force her breathing manually. Kyra's chest heaved at the first touch of his fingertips; she dragged in a deep breath and released it in a scream of delight. He sighed in relief that she hadn't succumbed again.

The tear beckoned, and Steden brushed it from Kyra's cheek, kissing her tenderly. "You are so beautiful," he mused. She was perfect, moreso than he'd dreamed, by far.

Kyra stared at him, silent, unreadable. His heart pounded in stark terror of what her reaction would be when she started sorting her thoughts and emotions about this turn of events.

The door to the stable crashed open, and Kyra shied, seeking further shelter behind his body, one hand covering her half-bared breasts, visible through the damp, white silin tunic.

Steden swung his head around, prepared to do verbal battle, going still at the sight of Michael Hi. Kyra's father stood, frozen in the doorway, his eyes locked on them. Confusion gave way to concern and fury alternating in his shifting expression.

For a moment, none of them moved. Kyra stared up at Steden, her breathing harsh. Steden lay locked in her band, one hand resting against her cheek and his eyes assessing Michael.

"Michael Hi?" Taven asked, breathing heavily. Steden's father pushed past Michael, his gaze panning over their locked bodies as if at a loss. "What in Len's Underworld—"

"I think that's obvious," Michael growled. "Mag's Justice, get off of her, boy."

Steden groaned at the reality of the situation. "That may...take a moment. Could we—uh—have a few—"

"Steden," his father warned. "This is not the time for levity."

"Oh, I am deadly serious, Father."

Michael stepped a stride toward them, his hands fisting. "Deadly is not a word I would use lightly, Steden." There was something more than a warning couched in that, perhaps a promise of assurances to be dealt.

"Please, leave," Kyra whispered.

"Kyra?" her father asked.

"This is the second time—" She took a calming breath and shook her head as if in decision. "Leave me." She waved her hand at both of their fathers as if in dismissal. "Both of you, get out."

Michael nodded curtly. "As you wish." He met Steden's eyes but spoke to his daughter. "I won't be far...if you need me—"

"I won't," she answered.

Taven pulled at Michael's shoulder, easing him out of the stable and closing the door behind them.

Steden sighed as his cock began to subside. "I'm sorry. I wanted—"

Kyra eased away, suddenly wary. He nodded, grinding his teeth as he left her body. She straightened her clothes with shaking hands, not meeting Steden's eyes.

Taking her lead, he dressed, assessing her every move. Would Kyra leave him? Would she ever forgive him for this? He hoped the answers to those questions were 'no' and 'very quickly.'

She glanced at him then away again, tucking her hair behind her ear. "I a-apologize for m-my father," she stammered. "H-he's a little protective."

"I would be, too," he warned her.

Kyra turned to him, at a loss for words.

Steden touched her cheek, heartened that she didn't move away. "I never meant to hurt or embarrass you. I let myself get carried away."

She nodded. "Would you..." Kyra twisted her fingers nervously.

"Yes?" he asked. That beginning sounded of something momentous.

"I want you to father my child."

He chuckled. "I already agreed to that," he reminded her. "I'm still willing."

"No. I don't mean a mechanical implantation, Steden. I want—" She blushed, lowering her face.

"You want a natural child? Maybe a daughter?"

She nodded.

Steden took a calming breath. It would take weeks...maybe months to produce a child that way. That was a lot of time to convince Kyra to more than a child.

He stroked her neck. "Yes. I'll give you a child." *I'll give you nearly anything you want.*

Kyra met his gaze, blinking back tears. "Thank you."

He nodded, biting back all the endearments he wanted to add to it...for now.

She pushed to her feet, shifting nervously from foot to foot. "I guess I better tell my father."

Steden swallowed a groan at the possible answers the prince might have to the idea.

* * * *

Steden sighed as Kyra stiffened in his arms. "We don't have to stay here," he offered. Perhaps her father's lake house was too remote. Perhaps she needed the feeling of being surrounded by her family while she experimented with reclaiming her sexuality.

She shook her head. "No. I don't want my father hovering." She scowled. "Or—Mag forbid!—*your* father."

"Mine," he finished along with her, gleaning her meaning without hesitation.

Kyra's unwillingness to breed naturally had been a terrible blow to the Breeding Office. Re-bred females were still too rare and precious to lose their participation in the process. Any chance to gain daughters from her would be seen as a gift, and Taven was hardly known for his patience.

Even if it hadn't been his son attempting to convince Kyra, Taven would be hard pressed to sit back and let it pass without interference.

Kyra blushed. "I don't know how to do this," she admitted miserably. "I've never—"

Of course she had, which was the problem. The schaen had scarred her for the act, and her body's weakness wasn't helping matters. All told, it was a work of Fion that she'd agreed to try again after her breathing problems in the stable.

Steden caressed his lips along the curve of hers, smiling when she didn't pull away. There was a chance for them yet. "You know," he whispered. "Your body knows. You felt the hunger in the stable. You followed it perfectly."

"Then why am I failing now?" She looked hopelessly lost.

"You're uncomfortable."

"And how—"

Steden started unbuttoning her trouskit. Kyra gasped, pushing at his hands.

"Shhh," he soothed her. "It's not what you think." He pushed the trouskit down her hips.

Kyra shifted nervously as they pooled around her ankles. "What are you doing?" There was just a hint of musk mingling into her scent. She was intrigued but not enough to call it arousal.

"Making you comfortable." Steden tugged at the ties on her tunic.

"But—" She gasped at the highest two ties popping free in unison.

Steden didn't give her a chance to protest. He stripped off the tunic and guided Kyra to the bed. Once he'd gotten her settled on the edge of the mattress, he sank to his knees before her. Her eyes widened, and her scent increased slightly. She was excited but too frightened to encourage him.

He raised one leg, and her fist settled on his shoulder, her breathing ragged. Kyra likely expected him to drink at her body, but that wasn't going to calm her. She had to be comfortable with him first. Passion would come later.

Her boot slid away with his hand, and her fist uncurled against his skin, her fingers massaging at the muscles at the back of his shoulder, testing his feel. Steden switched sides, removing her other boot. Kyra's exploring hand traced his bicep slowly.

When she was nude, he rose up over her. She leaned away, seemingly alarmed by the move. Steden offered a smile then lifted her onto the bed, drawing the silin sheets and quilts over her.

Her brow furrowed. "I don't..." Her voice hitched as Steden dragged his tunic over his head and tossed it onto the pile of her clothing.

He paused to allow her time to settle to the idea of him nude. When she didn't offer an expression or motion he could hope to interpret, Steden brushed a hand over the taut muscles of his abdomen, drawing her eyes to it.

Kyra bit her lip lightly, ranging her gaze over his chest and belly slowly. She met his eyes, questioning his intent silently. Steden toed off his boots, watching her for a nervous retreat that never came, then reached for the buttons on his trousers.

Kyra's eyes widened, and her color darkened. She wrapped an arm over her chest, locking the quilt to herself like a shield.

Steden cleared his throat, bringing her gaze back to his face. He held it there, stripping off his trousers without fanfare. He didn't move, waiting for some sign of her acceptance. She seemed frozen in place for a hand of heartbeats.

Her eyes flicked up and down, focusing her gaze on his face, then his length, returning to his face just as quickly. She drew in a slow, steady breath, then trailed her gaze down again, examining his half-erect cock at length. Her arm eased away, signaling her acceptance of his state of undress.

He smiled, crossing to the far side of the bed and sliding beneath the quilts with her. Kyra met his eyes, wary again, her arm tightening.

"A man can lay with a woman without mating," he assured her. "Just lay with me."

Kyra opened her mouth as if to speak then closed it, the furrows in her brow cutting deep.

Steden touched her cheek. "Your parents share a bed," he noted. "Do you think they mate every time they lay in it together?" He hoped she wouldn't reply with a comment about the mother's fast.

She didn't. "Of course not. But...don't you want to?" Her lack of confidence seared him.

"With every cell in my body, but mating isn't dependent on the wishes of one person. There are two involved, Kyra. That is why we're going to lay together without more today."

"But I asked you to—"

He leaned across her and brushed his lips over her hair.

"We...we already have," she stammered.

"Do you remember the frenzy?" he asked. "Do you remember how free you were in the stable?"

"Yes." Her scent deepened, proof that she wanted what she was asking for...on some level.

On some level wasn't good enough. Steden returned to his side of the bed. "That is when you offer yourself. Tonight is not a time you will. If you wish to lie in my arms, I'm here for you. If you don't wish it, I will understand your reluctance. This has been a whirlwind change for you."

Kyra turned to her side, watching him as if there was some puzzle in his words. Her eyes grew heavy. Soon, she was sound asleep next to him.

Steden sighed. He was halfway to his goal: sleeping in Kyra's bed, enjoying her body, and slowly earning her trust. He just hoped there was a chance of reaching the greatest reward—her love.

CHAPTER TWENTY-THREE

Zor 4, Ri 25-3017

"I don't understand what purpose this serves," Kyra complained, trying to cover herself with a sheet.

Steden rolled his eyes and gathered her hands in his own. "Do you ever want to attempt to conceive your daughter?" he asked pointedly.

She blushed, her body heating at the prospect of experiencing Steden again. Kyra closed her eyes, letting the memories of his possession wash over her.

For two days, she'd wanted him again, but Steden seemed intent on driving her to madness.

He insisted on nudity for much of the day. Kyra wasn't finding herself more at ease with her own nudity as the days passed, but she was more than content with Steden's. The staff of his ready length was the stuff of dreams, and he encouraged her to touch any and all of him she cared to.

Steden pulled her to his body, his scent surrounding her and that hard ridge pressing into her hip. His fingertips stroked a peaked nipple.

Kyra gasped in surprise. He released her immediately, his face reflecting his frustration and hers for a heartbeat before he pasted on a wry smile.

"In time," he managed in a rough voice. "You'll come to trust me in time."

She bit back a sob. All Kyra wanted was Steden, but she feared him at the same time. "Massage me," she requested, at a loss for any other way to urge her body into a mindless response.

His brow furrowed, and his eyes narrowed. "You're sore?"

Kyra shook her head. "In the stable..." It was no use. Voicing the reasoning that she'd succumbed that way once was impossible.

"You want me to help trick your mind into accepting me?"

"Yes. I don't understand myself, Steden. I want you...not just logically...for a child. I want—" She pressed her hand to the heavy ache in her abdomen. "I feel it. I do. I just..."

Steden smiled. "There are better ways to convince you, if you wish to be convinced," he offered.

"What do you mean?" *Not the musk alone*, she pleaded. That hadn't gone well the first time, and she certainly didn't want to repeat the experience.

"You know I'm an implanted re-bred," he reminded her.

"Of course." It made him a viable donor to her child, after all. "What does that—"

"The healing magic," he prodded, as if that meant something to Kyra.

She searched her scant memories of the lessons she'd had before the schaen, coming up with no connection. "What does that have to do with mating?"

His eyes widened in surprise. "You don't know?"

Kyra stiffened her spine, on the defensive that quickly, her anger rising for a fight. "They didn't continue my mating studies after the...incident," she supplied crisply. "Why would they?"

Steden groaned. "They should have, for your protection, if for no other reason." His expression softened, and he reached out to trail a fingertip down the line of her jaw from ear to chin. "You are so innocent." He hesitated a moment. "Would you like to learn?"

Her heart rate jumped to a staccato beat not unlike the dance of the spring festival. She nodded, words failing her when she needed them most, when she needed to ask questions, when she longed to beg him to touch her.

He took her hand in his, leading Kyra to the bed. She started to raise her leg, preparing to stretch out on the mattress, but Steden stilled her, shaking his head.

"Not yet," he whispered. Instead, he pulled her to his body, burying his face in Kyra's neck.

She closed her eyes, willing her body not to clench as Steden kissed at the pulse point in the hollow of her throat. Kyra swallowed down a sob, wishing she could find the peace she'd known in the stable, wishing she—

The sensation of ice came first, stronger than she remembered it. The cold shot over her nerves, and her whole body hummed in a strange sort of anticipation.

Kyra tangled her fingers in Steden's hair as ice became fire, a wild conflagration that was almost painful in its intensity. Steden leaned back, meeting her gaze steadily, waiting.

Waiting for what?

Her knees buckled, her hands clenching in his hair. The pleasure coursing through her made her mind spin.

Steden supported her, lowering Kyra to the bed then following her down. His lips brushed over her inner wrist, sending ice to overlap the reaction still holding her in its thrall.

His mouth covered hers, muting her cry of surrender. Kyra shook her head as Steden retreated. She didn't want him to leave her; she wanted him to fill the void he'd created so simply.

Steden guided her hands from his hair as he eased away from her. She murmured a protest. He couldn't leave her now. He couldn't—

Kyra bowed up to him, as ice spread from a point on her abdomen and through her womb. "No," she pleaded, gleaning what was coming next. "Not yet."

She gasped at the burn, making her hunger for him more acute. Kyra screamed at the jolt of pleasure sending her over.

Steden covered her with a groan, his cock parting her entrance and stretching her body wide around him. He slid his forearms under her knees, lifting Kyra's lower body from the bed and spreading her open for his thrusts.

He was relentless, his body lodging so deep with each forward roll of his hips that Steden lifted more of her back from the surface of the mattress. His hips beat like a drum on her inner thighs, and the similarity to the spring dance resonated in her muddled mind again.

They say the Keen learned that dance from the Sivrah. They say the Sivrah still practice fertility ceremonies. It was likely a lie, but that was what the tales reported to those who cared to listen.

He met her gaze, his expression fierce. Kyra shivered, praying Steden wouldn't proclaim her his, as the schaen had. She had to believe he was different. She had to know it.

Steden lodged deep inside her, a growl issuing from between clenched teeth as his seed bathed the sensitized gates of her womb. It was a hot, potent wave that might give her a daughter of her own.

She stilled as he locked into the band, fighting to make her body function. Memories of her panic with the schaen...of her body's failure to function when her egg released, washed over her. She battled them back as she had in the stable, trembling in the effort.

Steden released her knees, cupping her face in one large hand. "It's me," he soothed her. "Look in my eyes, Kyra. It's just me."

Kyra drew in a deeper breath, forcing her tight chest muscles to move more naturally. It hurt, but it wasn't impossible. She groaned, her awareness of the continuing shocks of her release drowning out the discomfort and forcing her breathing to ease.

"That's right," Steden urged her. "Do you feel the egg? Is my seed filling your womb?"

It was. The heat made her feel as if she'd been transported to the soul's reward.

This was the reason she'd asked Steden to share her bed. The chance of a daughter had never been enough to entice her before, because she'd never felt this part of the climax she'd had with the schaen. It was a sensation Kyra wished she could hold to.

"It feels good, doesn't it?" he breathed.

Kyra nodded, tracing her fingertips over the lines of his chest. "Again," she begged.

Steden smiled. "It's difficult for you to accept the stimulation. It's not wise to tire you with it, until you adjust to the sensation. You'll be ready for me again soon."

And that quickly, her arousal faded. Her stomach lurched. Kyra looked away, her heart pounding a new non-rhythm that made her smoothing breathing catch again.

He turned her chin back gently, his expression concerned. "What is it? What did I do wrong?"

"Nothing," she lied. "It was nothing."

"It was not nothing," he insisted. "I do not want to hurt you, Kyra. You must talk to me."

Kyra felt her cheeks heat. She'd spoken to no one about the schaen. If she didn't talk to her mother and sisters, she certainly couldn't speak to Steden about it.

She shook her head slowly, refusing him.

"Someday, you'll trust me," he repeated.

CHAPTER TWENTY-FOUR

Zor 7, Ri 25-3017

Steden sighed at the sight of the women exiting the transport. Michael had given his vow not to hover over Kyra, but he hadn't promised not to send her female relatives to make certain his middle daughter was well and happy.

"We should dress," he informed her, trying to hide his irritation.

"Why?" Her hand traced the line of his shoulder.

Kyra had been touching him more and more often of late, her aversion to exploring Steden's body fading slowly, though unexpected touches still startled her, no matter how they occurred.

Her fingers drifted down his spine, caressing the curve of his buttocks, and he hardened in response. Kyra's breasts pressed to his back; her lips brushed over the back of his neck, parted, and her tongue made delicious little circles over the nerve bundle.

He groaned. "Mag alive! I want you." But they were about to be interrupted.

Kyra circled his body. She traced the line of curls from his chest to his hungry length. At the prompting, his cock bobbed toward her, straining toward its happy retreat home in her body.

"You say that like it's a bad thing," she noted in a slightly-tremulous but breathy voice.

Steden guided her toward the bed, shaking his head. "It's not." *I wish you wanted me like this every moment.*

He captured her lips beneath his and swept Kyra down onto the silin sheets. She met him, her lips and tongue ravenous, pressing her mound up to him, begging Steden to come inside.

This was what he wanted. This was how he wanted her—alive and passionate.

Her family could wait. Her father could serve a time in Len's Dungeons, for all Steden cared.

He surged into her, his groan rumbling and mixing with hers. Fion, but he needed this. "I will always want you," he breathed against her lips.

Kyra's eyes opened wide. She looked at him in something resembling confusion, opened her mouth to speak...and made no sound, whatsoever.

A brisk knock made Steden falter in his smooth thrusts. "Go away," he growled.

"The lady's mother and sisters wait to see her, mi'lord. I will see to their comforts."

Kyra pushed at his chest, looking panicked. "We have to stop," she pleaded.

"We don't," he insisted. "They can wait a few—"

"No. Please." Her lip trembled, and she looked close to tears.

He nodded, stilling inside her, smiling wryly at the flutter of her inner muscles clenching lightly around him. She wasn't still; Kyra's hips rocked minutely, a seemingly unconscious move. Steden didn't doubt it would be easy enough to get her back in this position once her family left.

For now, retreat was called for, but it was a momentary withdrawal. "As you wish. When you're ready—"

She winced.

"What did I—"

"Nothing," Kyra gasped. "Please, Steden."

He nodded, brushing his lips over hers as he left her body. Steden helped Kyra to her feet, unsurprised when she all but bolted to the cabinet and started to dress. He followed her example, trying to catalog what caused such troubling reactions in her.

Still lost in thought, Steden crossed the room and straightened her gown. Kyra stiffened, shooting him a nervous glance in the mirror. He eased his hands away, gritting his teeth at this new setback. He followed her to her family, careful not to touch her again.

Diran met Steden's eyes as they entered, blushed, then rushed to Kyra for a hug. "How are you?" she asked urgently.

Kyra nodded, managing a strained smile. "Very well, Diran. Thank you for asking."

Steden noted Kyra's rigid posture. He wanted to soothe her, but he'd upset her somehow. It would take time and patience to ease her fears and calm Kyra to the idea of approaching him again.

Danellan came next, gathering Kyra in her arms and shooting Steden an encouraging smile.

"Father sent you, didn't he?" Kyra asked with a nervous laugh.

"No," her mother protested. "Of course not."

"Yes," Gibril countered in obvious glee.

Danellan shot her eldest daughter a scathing look. "Really, Gibril," she chided. "His grumbling about promising not to come himself had nothing to do with my decision to come."

Gibril smiled a sickeningly sweet little smile that was completely at odds with her personality. "Of course, Mother. If you'll excuse me, I am ravenous. I believe I'll seek out a snack." She sauntered out the far doorway like a jaglin bitch on the prowl for a mate.

Diran shook her head. "Gibby lives on her stomach. If it weren't for her other amusements, she'd match a war-buck in mass."

"Dirry." There was a note of exasperation in Danellan's voice that Steden rarely heard from her. "Don't be unkind."

"Really, Mother. Her only loves are food, riding, and men."

"Two of those are of a type," Kyra mused. She clapped a hand over her mouth, shooting Steden a wild-eyed look, her face darkening at Diran's snicker.

He nodded, a sudden realization taking hold. "I will leave you to speak in peace," he offered, exiting with a quick bow to each woman.

Steden made his way to the kitchen, waving the cooks and servants away so that he could converse with Gibril in private.

She met his eyes with a mischievous little smile, taking a bite of a ripe lizor berry that could nearly be described as indecent. "I thought you might seek me out," she spoke around the bit of berry. Gibril chewed and swallowed, her gaze taking his measure. "Is it going that badly?" She seemed smug.

"The schaen certainly didn't leave her with trust for men," he admitted. Steden couldn't think of it as confiding, since he didn't delude himself that Gibril was one to keep her lips sealed.

Gibril laughed shortly. "Though few people believe it, the schaen did nothing to cause this. He was wonderful. Kyra simply...wasn't made for romps."

Steden shook off his shock and pushed back his fury. It was obvious Gibril knew nothing about Kyra; she was a passionate lover when she made it past the pitfield of her past experience.

She glided to him, her fingertips tracing the waistband of his trousers. "Poor Steden. I can help you relieve what my sister won't."

He pushed her hand away, repulsed and confused at once. "I am not a schaen," he reminded her.

Gibril's smile widened. "I use Walla teas when I wish to escape schaen. I like escaping them often." She pressed her body to his. "There is something special about a whole man."

Steden eased away from her, ignoring Gibril's pout. "Tell me about the schaen who took Kyra's barrier," he ordered.

"Why?" Her eyes glittered in curiosity.

"You were there. You know what he did. You know the things he said to her."

Gibril bristled. "He did nothing wrong," she insisted hotly.

"Whether he did or not, his actions scarred Kyra. I need to know those scars to get past them."

She shrugged, seemingly only mildly mollified. "I don't know what to tell you. Kyra enjoyed every touch, until she succumbed. He touched her, kissed her...drank at her body."

"Did Kyra seek him out?"

"I don't know what you mean." But she averted her eyes, a sure sign that he'd been right to ask...and that she did know precisely what he meant.

Steden growled in frustration at her evasion. "Did Kyra ask you to have your schaen take her barrier?" He doubted it. Kyra would have done it correctly.

Gibril turned away, winding her fingers in the short skirt of her dress nervously.

"She didn't," Steden decided.

"It was a gift. I gave the best of my schaen to her as a gift," Gibril whispered. She'd undoubtedly used that defense before.

"Why didn't she ask for a woman healer? How did he convince her to forego tradition and safety?"

Gibril snorted. "There was no convincing involved."

"You mean he took her unwilling," he growled.

She turned back to him, her painted eyes wide. "No. Of course not, but Kyra's mating frenzy was at a fever before I sent him to her. She all but threw herself at him."

"You used an aphrodisiac on her?" That was illegal.

"Are you insane? Why would I do that?"

Steden rubbed at the stiffness in the back of his neck. "Mating frenzy? But without an aphrodisiac or someone touching her..." It made no sense.

"I had her hide and watch while two schaen played at me. I took the other and ordered Kyra's gift to prepare himself for her. I imagine the musk and her watching..." Gibril shrugged.

"You let him take her that way? It's no wonder she doesn't trust men. What were you thinking?"

She stiffened. "I thought she would enjoy herself, and she did, I assure you. Were it not for her frailty, she would have remembered that day fondly for the rest of her life."

"The problem is, Gibril," he ground out from between clenched teeth, "she never *has* forgotten it. Now, what did your favorite schaen do to her? What did he say?"

"He mastered her. Oh, he was respectful about it, but Kyra gave herself to him completely. It was rather interesting, really. I mean, women don't usually give themselves over to schaen that way. They are there to serve us, after all."

"She was unschooled," he protested. "Kyra wasn't ready."

"I was unschooled. I never—"

"Kyra is not you," Steden snapped. *Thank Fion for that!*

Gibril chuckled, smoothing the front of his tunic. "I could make that clear to you," she offered.

Steden brushed her hand away. "The only thing I want from you is answers. What did he say to her? What did he do...precisely?"

She shrugged. "Then we each have something of value to the other."

"Do we?"

Gibril nodded, a sly little vixen smile curving her painted lips.

"So, you have the information I seek to offer."

The smile widened.

"And just what do I have to offer you?" His gut twisted in apprehension. Surely, even Gibril wouldn't dare—

She did. Her fingertips traced the line of his flaccid cock through his trousers. "A diversion."

Steden yanked her hand away, making a conscious effort not to snap her wrist in anger. "I will find out my own way," he growled.

Gibril's eyes widened in surprise, and her face paled behind the powder and rouge. "You're refusing me?" There was something dangerous in that, something with an edge of laser blue.

"Yes, he is."

Steden turned to Kyra, only vaguely aware that he still held Gibril's wrist in his fisted hand.

* * * *

Kyra couldn't seem to control her trembling. *How dare she! How dare Gibril—* She pushed away an image of Steden's body pounding into Gibril's as her sister's schaen had, Gibril leaned over the counter or table instead of the foot of her bed.

"Kyra," Gibril greeted her calmly, moving her hand as if to remind Steden to release her.

Steden startled, pushing Gibril's hand away. He took a step toward Kyra. "You know I would never—"

"I know very well what happened here," she interrupted him.

Gibril plucked a slice of cheese from the tray at her side, seemingly unaffected. The woman had no shame.

Kyra turned for the door. "Give Mother my regards, Gibril. Perhaps it would be best if you didn't visit unannounced anymore."

"Going somewhere?" Gibril asked.

Kyra paused, taking Steden's hand and urging him along with her. "I have something to discuss with Steden. I trust you can find your way out, once you finish eating."

"Len's Underworld, Kyra! The man—"

"Is mine, for as long as he sleeps in my bed," Kyra snapped, turning her head to shoot a venomous look at her elder sister. "I don't share men with you. I learned long ago that our tastes vary too widely for that."

Gibril gaped at her, for once forgetting her various hungers and seemingly at a loss for words consecutively. Steden looked from Gibril to Kyra, clearly biting back laughter, his eyes crinkled in amusement.

Kyra looked away, inexplicably close to tears. Steden was here to give Kyra the heir she wanted. Nothing more. Why would Kyra care that Gibril wanted him?

She left the kitchen with Steden trailing in her wake, troubled.

Perhaps it was simply Gibril's timing. When Kyra had her heir, Steden would be free to go to any bed he wished.

Kyra faltered at the wave of pain that thought caused her. She pressed a shaking hand to the tightness around her lungs. Steden *was* free to move on. Kyra had no hold on him.

"What is it?" he asked.

She shook her head, stiffening as his hand came to rest on the small of her back.

Kyra swallowed hard, blinking back tears. Steden couldn't even touch her without her reacting badly to it. Why would Kyra try to hold him to her? To taunt him with something she could never be? To have a friend near, when any normal male required more?

No. When her heir was secure, Steden would move on to what every male of their race wanted, a responsive bride and a house full of strong children. Trying to hold him would be selfish.

Kyra pushed through the door to their room, releasing his hand, sick in the knowledge that Gibril was right about her. The snide comments over the years were correct. Kyra was frail; her body had failed her...then her mind had, if the latest tests were sound.

Steden closed the door. "What is it?" he asked. He paused, continuing in a voice that was hesitant...perhaps hopeful, but she couldn't guess what he hoped for. "You must know I'd never bed Gibril."

She turned to him, crossed the room, and pulled his face down for a searing kiss. Her heart ached. How could she want him so much and fear him, at the same time?

He groaned, breaking off the kiss. "You don't have to do this," Steden soothed her. "Not like this. You have nothing to prove."

Kyra shook her head, laying a kiss on the pulse point at his throat, opening the ties on his tunic.

Steden shivered, his hands skating over her spine. "Don't do this because of Gibril," he pleaded.

"I'm not." *I hope I'm not.* But Kyra wasn't certain about that.

She opened his trousers and stroked his rigid member.

"Kyra." It came out a hoarse whisper.

She knelt before him, taking Steden into her mouth. The motion was awkward at first, but Kyra soon found a rhythm and position that proved comfortable.

Steden's hands cupped the back of her skull, guiding her mouth up and down the length of his cock. "I'm going to drink at you. The moment you've had enough of me, I'm going to drink at you."

Heat pooled in Kyra's womb. As if Steden sensed it, his body responded with a slight release of his musk into her mouth. She groaned, closing her eyes, her fingers easing the ache in her hood through the silin of her gown.

"Let me take you to the bed," he pleaded.

Kyra released him, licking at the cleft in the head. "No," she whispered. "Let me taste you."

"We can taste each other."

"After." A niggling of a memory teased at her muddled mind. "The musk is an aphrodisiac."

"Oh, yes." It wasn't confirmation that she'd remembered the information correctly. Steden wanted that.

Kyra sucked him deep into her mouth again, ruthlessly driving him toward his climax. Steden's hand tangled in her hair, and his muscles tightened down, but he didn't force her into the rhythm he wanted.

Her name left his lips on whisper after whisper. At last, they grew more ragged, louder... Then he was shouting her name, his seed filling her mouth. Kyra swallowed reflexively, and Steden shouted again, encouraging her.

She repeated the swallowing motion, again and again, while he thickened in her mouth. Kyra stilled, trying to recreate the sensation of climax inside her for him.

"No." Steden guided her head back and forth. "Like you were..." He was panting, coated in sweat.

Kyra went back to the swallowing motions, suckling at him, shallow and deep.

"Gods, yes," he breathed. "Anything. Name anything."

The fire raging low in her belly demanded his cock, pounding hard. But he'd need time to recover after this encounter. *Won't he?*

As if in confirmation, his cock subsided.

Steden didn't waste a moment. He guided her to her feet then toward the bed, pulling up at her dress.

"You're going to drink," she reminded herself.

"I am." He inhaled deeply. "And you're so sweet and hot for it."

Kyra sank to the edge of the mattress, spreading her legs wide for him, her sex radiating heat, just as he'd said it was. "Will it make you ready again?" She vaguely remembered something about mating frenzies caused by sharing musk.

Steden drew her hand to his cock. It was hard and weeping. "Just your scent does. Drinking you is going to make me..."

"What? What will it do?"

"If you choose not to take me afterward, I'll have to relieve myself." He paused, cocking his head to one side. "Would you like to watch me do that?"

A vivid memory of the schaen stroking himself in preparation for her assaulted her mind. "No."

Steden nodded, sinking to his knees. That was enough to banish the memory. Kyra shifted her legs wider, her breathing hitching at his slow approach.

"Watch what I do to you."

His hands came up, parting her slit, allowing the cool room air to stroke at the heated flesh between. Steden blew lightly, taunting her. His tongue followed, flicking inside. Kyra jumped in response, and Steden started to pull away. She clasped the back of his head, urging him toward her again.

He was relentless. With her encouragement, Steden was passion unleashed. Kyra watched him, her body rioting. He drank like a man parched from desert ops. He feasted like a man starved from survival training in the Garesh Mountains...or a man deprived of a woman for too long.

He has been. He's been with me.

That sobering thought couldn't stand long against his attentions. Her breathing degraded to sharp little gasps, and moans escaped her. Pressure and pleasure warred, buffeting each other within her until Kyra felt she could stand no more. Then she was soaring, weightless, pushed on waves of warmth and jostled by fierce hungers.

Her senses cleared enough to note that she'd collapsed to the mattress, one leg wrapped around Steden's body. He was on his knees between her legs, his cock just a little lower than they would need to make love in this position. Kyra tightened her leg, drawing him closer.

"Are you sure?" he asked.

"Certain. Absolutely certain."

Steden climbed onto the bed, sliding her back along the silin sheets, pulling her legs over his and positioning her sheath for him. He didn't thrust deep, as she expected. Instead, he toyed with her, pushing in just far enough to fire her inner pleasure spot.

Kyra wriggled against him, trying to push Steden deeper. He took a finger-width more...then another...more with each forward roll of his hips.

"More," she gasped.

"More?"

"Don't stop."

He did.

"Steden—"

"Touch yourself, Kyra. Touch where we join."

Her hand trembling, she did as he ordered, slipping her fingers between her thighs, pausing for a moment at her hood.

"That's right. It feels good to touch while I love you. Doesn't it?" His voice was seduction itself.

Kyra circled her hood, moaning at the combined pleasure of being stretched around Steden's cock and her own hand working her while he watched.

"Now where we're joined."

His cock was slick with her fluids, hard against the softness of her slit, pulsing beneath her hand. She felt it jerk, inside and out.

Steden started moving, back and forth. Kyra started to ease her hand away, and he captured it and held it to him.

"What does it feel like, Kyra?"

She fumbled for words in her unresponsive mind, finally settling for the most inane thing imaginable. "Good. So good."

His hips pushed faster and deeper. "Yes, it does."

Though he released her hand to position her for a smoother journey, Kyra held it there, feeling him thrust until she felt their intimate curls on either side of her fingers, withdrawing coated in her musk.

It felt right. Natural. Steden belonged sheathed inside her.

That thought shot her to climax...and Steden with her. She'd barely noted the explosion of her egg when her breathing failed her. Her chest tightened, and she panicked, grabbing for his shoulder. One breath escaped her...and she greedily grabbed for another. And another.

Her heart ached. No matter how right it felt, Steden belonged sheathed inside a woman who wouldn't fail him sexually, and there was no question that she would. Tears blurred her vision, and for once, she didn't try to stem the flow.

CHAPTER TWENTY-FIVE

Zor 9, Ri 25-3017

Kyra glanced at Steden from beneath her eyelashes. He ate his meal in silence, not looking at her, his body tense.

Steden hadn't touched her in two days, ever since the deplorable crying fit she'd indulged in. Kyra hadn't realized how much she'd miss it.

How much will I miss it when I know I'll never share a bed with him again?

"You should eat, Kyra," he noted.

She placed her fork on the table.

"Not hungry?" he asked.

Kyra traced a finger up his thigh, biting her lip lightly as his cock hardened in response. She was hungry, ravenous for his body.

"My way," he whispered.

"Anything," she vowed.

Steden met her gaze steadily, setting his fork aside. He turned in his chair, grasping the edge of her chair and easing it around until she faced him. Kyra looked to the bed in confusion.

"No," he whispered.

She watched in amazement as he hooked his hands behind her knees and pulled her to the edge of the chair, spreading her legs around his.

"How can we," she began, breaking off in surprise as his fingers teased at her core.

It felt wonderful, and yet— "But Steden, I want—"

"My way," he rasped.

"Yes."

"Gods but you're beautiful."

He took his time, stroking her body, inside and out, exploring every finger-width, his eyes heavy in desire. Her body ached for him, her nipples coming to points, her womb hot and heavy. Kyra pressed a hand to her stomach, rubbing at the tightness.

"Touch yourself." His breath was hot against her mouth.

"How? Like I did when we—"

"Yes. Bring yourself over."

Her stomach clenched. Bring herself over? While he watched?

"What is it?" he murmured. "There was something the schaen did, wasn't there?"

She started to deny it, then reconsidered. How many times had she shied because Steden did something that set her teeth on edge? It was time to take charge of what she wanted. That meant doing the one thing she never had...talking to someone about what went on that day.

"Yes. Gibril...had him prepare himself for me. He...stroked himself while she and the other—"

Steden leaned toward her and laid a gentle kiss on her lips. "Perhaps someday that will loosen its grip on you. Until then, I will keep it in mind."

She nodded, grateful that she'd decided to trust him with the information.

"Now, what other things should I be aware of? I know that being interrupted disturbs you. I understand why."

Kyra took a calming breath. "Do not..."

"Yes?"

"Do not ask me if I am ready for you."

He hesitated, seemingly committing it to memory, then nodded.

She rushed on, a heady sense of security and accomplishment driving her. "And do not claim me."

His brow furrowed. "Claim you? How do you mean that?"

The schaen's words echoed in her mind.

"Kyra, I will endeavor to do anything you require to be at ease, but I have to know specifically what was said or done to cause the unease."

She nodded, forcing another deep breath. "Do not..."

Steden nodded his encouragement.

"Do not proclaim me yours...as if you owned me."

His smile widened. "I will do my best to remember it."

* * * *

The information changed his plan, but it was better that he know than not. Steden drew Kyra onto his lap and turned her away from him. That left them both facing the mirror.

"Did you enjoy watching me drink from you?" he inquired.

"Yes."

"And feeling my cock moving in and out of you?"

"Oh, yes."

"Good." Steden hesitated, deliberating how much advance preparation to give her. *A lot. More is better than less with Kyra.*

He played a finger inside her, smiling at her groan. "Watch in the mirror, Kyra. Watch me touch you. When you wish to feel my length, say it."

She stiffened at the suggestion, then did as he bid. In moments, she was eased against his body.

Steden added a second finger. A moment later, he started using his other hand to tease her nipples up. Kyra moaned, shifting her hips to work his fingers deeper.

Her eyes slid shut, and she threw her head side to side, gasping out pleas for more. Steden could have insisted she keep watching, but an enjoyable experience was more important to his ultimate plan.

"I want it," she whispered.

"What do you want?" he replied.

"I want you to make love to me."

Steden didn't waste time. He eased his fingers out of her, lifted Kyra slightly and guided her down onto his cock.

"Yes. Oh, yes," she breathed.

"Watch, Kyra. See what we look like together."

Her eyes slid open, and Steden started moving, slowly at first then faster. The mirror was perfect. In it, he could see every finger-width of his cock moving in and out of her tight little body. He could see her look of fascination, the way her face contorted in her coming climax, the scream of release working up her throat.

Kyra reached back and fisted one hand in his hair, her screams echoing off the walls, her body milking his to climax. The fight for air followed on the heels of his cock locking into the band. It was better than some nights, worse than others.

In the aftermath, Kyra's expression crumpled into a complex mix of guilt and misery.

Someday, he vowed. Someday, she'd come to accept that he didn't see her condition the same way.

CHAPTER TWENTY-SIX

Zor 31, Ri 25-3017

Kyra wandered the storefronts, pausing at the nursery store. She took a step toward the door...then hesitated.

She wasn't carrying. At this speed, Kyra might never carry. It was still only one day in two or three that she could finish a sexual encounter, and the odds hadn't caught up with her yet.

Not like they have for that other woman.

Kyra winced at the bitter thought. The woman in question was a lowborn having problems with her fifth child. They'd called on Steden to aid her, which was how Kyra had ended up wandering the marketplace.

Even teeming with servants, the house had felt empty and cold. *Without Steden.*

That thought was too distressing to follow further. It was safer to think about his current task.

Five children! Granted, her own mother and Aunt Susan had five each, but with the reforms her father had passed, few lowborn had more than two or three.

The nursery window drew her gaze again, and her attention darted from one design of quilt to another. Purchasing one before she carried seemed to court Len's humor and invite ill will, so she didn't dare enter the store.

Five... What I wouldn't give for one. She cocked her head to one side, allowing herself to dream. *Or two. I wonder if Steden would agree—*

That's assuming we manage a first. Kyra sighed.

"You will. Your heart's desires and more."

She turned her head, and the riot of colors assaulted her eyes. *Sivrah.* "Pardon?" Kyra must have misheard the woman. Or perhaps, she had been speaking to someone else.

She's looking at me.

"Your ears have not deceived you, and I am speaking to you."

Kyra's heart pounded sickly, and she glanced around suspiciously.

"But you don't believe that." Her smile widened. "I didn't expect you would."

Kyra scowled. "You claim to be a telepath." She'd heard tales that there were people of such odd talents among the Sivrah. One of the many rumors about Pilar's husband was that he was secretly a Sivrah bastard.

The Sivrah tipped her head in affirmation. Her long, sleek hair swung around her young face.

A telepath. A trick is more likely. Kyra turned to go. "You don't have to be a telepath to reason that I want a child," she replied dryly. "I am looking into a nursery store window, after all."

"Ah, but a child isn't your heart's desire, is it?"

The comment stopped Kyra cold, and her mind went racing. "What do you mean?"

"Your man." The voice was closer, but Kyra didn't turn to it. "You said you'd never contract, but you want to. Don't you, mi'lady." It wasn't a question, and there was something irreverent in calling a Keen princess mi'lady, as if Kyra was a common noblewoman.

But she couldn't focus on her outrage, in light of the greater portion of the message. "Who told you that?" she gasped. Her heart skipped in a mind-spinning non-rhythm, but Kyra couldn't say why it did.

"You did." The Sivrah moved closer, whispering now. "You don't feel you can be a wife to him...the wife he deserves, but you can."

Tears stung at Kyra's eyes. "I can't," she managed bitterly. "Everything they've tried—"

"Ah, the Keen doctors. So concerned with their drugs, they've forgotten the simple cures Fion gifted us. A woman healer would—"

Kyra turned on her, coming face to face with the Sivrah woman, her fury igniting. "They've failed as well."

This close, she could see the strange color of the Sivrah's eyes. They seemed to glow like a jaglin's in firelight. The other woman's voice dragged her back to the conversation.

"Then they have forgotten what they once knew," she offered sadly.

"You're saying they simply...forgot something so important?"

A niggling of unease came with that thought. It was possible. Berel had forgotten the entire chapter on the subject of seduction. Since she considered it morally-unsound, she'd made no note of it...until Joseph used it. Could they have made no note of the cure for Kyra as well. It was a rare condition. How often would they have need of the knowledge?

"Or lost the knowledge. The woman healers had their wings clipped by Ro Ti. No woman healer has been permitted full knowledge of Mother Fion's ways since then." There was a telling pause. "Save Sivrah woman healers."

"Why would Sivrah woman healers have knowledge the Keen don't?"

The Sivrah turned and took a step away.

"Wait," Kyra ordered.

"We are drawing attention, young princess."

Kyra flicked a glance around, grinding her teeth at the curious looks being shot her way. She was so intent on a way to explain talking to a Sivrah that she almost missed the motion of the woman turning the corner.

Forcing a calming breath, Kyra feigned interest in the shop window. A moment later, she turned the opposite direction than the one the Sivrah had taken. At the next cross-street, she turned in.

A flash of brilliant color disappearing around another corner led her on. Kyra ambled along, pretending to consider a pair of lounging pants here and boots there.

The game continued across the marketplace and out into the park district. At last, Kyra caught sight of the woman; she was standing next to a large transport, speaking to one of her men.

The man's head swung toward Kyra, and he smiled, panning his gaze up and down her body. Kyra went still, her heart pounding again. She didn't know why she'd followed the Sivrah blindly.

No one knew she was here, and the stories said Sivrah weren't to be trusted.

The Sivrah woman smacked him soundly across his cheek. He lowered his eyes, darkening to crimson. She waved him back, then crossed the grass to Kyra.

"My apologies for my brother's rudeness," she offered.

Kyra backed off a step. "Perhaps I should—"

"You have questions."

She did, but Kyra wasn't certain she was safe here.

"Jotem."

The man rushed to her side, and Kyra took another step away. He didn't reach for her, didn't even look at her.

The Sivrah woman passed him something. "Bring Kyra Hir's driver," she ordered. She hurried on, cutting off Kyra's protest. "Tell the man the princess tired and gave you that coin to fetch him to her."

Before Kyra could question the lie, he was gone at a run. A heavy silence fell in his wake.

The Sivrah waved her toward a stone bench. "Will you sit?"

"Who are you?"

"My name is Velinda."

Kyra committed it to memory, nodded, and sat.

Velinda sat beside her, waiting for Kyra to organize her thoughts.

"Why would the Sivrah woman healers have more information than the Keen?"

She sighed, shifting position to draw her legs under her on the bench. "It is said the Sivrah were founded by the last true woman healers...the last of Fion's Children. While Ro Ti didn't permit his bride to teach the Magden woman healers all of Fion's secrets, and Juleron didn't allow his traitor bride to practice at all, a small number of young priestesses escaped Gidlore and founded the Sivrah, drawing men from refugees of the great war. Men who were willing to submit to the rule of their women, according to the ancient traditions."

"But—"

Velinda waved her off. "You have more important questions, and we have little time."

Kyra did have questions, but she didn't know where to begin.

"Do you wish a reprieve from your affliction?"

"Yes." It came out a gasp.

She nodded. "There is a simple herbal tea. Taken daily, it will stifle the response."

"What kind of tea?" How could something so elemental be lost? If Ro Ti did suppress some of the teachings, why would he suppress this?

"It contains powders of a dozen herbs. It is the mixture that matters." Velinda waved off Kyra's next question. "Your driver will arrive soon, and we don't have time to discuss the recipe."

"It will work?"

"It has never failed in a case like your own." She seemed sincere in that claim.

"And it's safe?"

"Completely."

There had to be some trick in this. Nothing was gained without some cost. *Cost!* "How much will such a miracle cost me?"

The Sivrah were dirt-poor migrant workers. They wore clothing made from the silin rags of the rich. Kyra braced herself for an outrageous sum to be quoted.

Will I pay it?

For the chance of a normal life with Steden, she'd pay almost any price.

Kyra stiffened, belatedly remembering that Velinda could hear her thoughts, as if she'd spoken aloud.

"I am a woman healer," Velinda replied crisply.

"Even a woman healer receives payment for her services."

Her features softened. "Five silver for the tea then."

"Five?" Kyra had expected to pay twenty times that amount, at a minimum. She'd been willing to pay a hundred times that sum for a cure.

"It is not a cure, but it will alleviate the difficulties for you. That will be enough to let you be the wife you wish to be to your man."

I've offended her. Would Velinda raise the price now? Kyra wasn't certain she'd care.

"Five silver," the Sivrah repeated.

"Done."

Velinda pulled a large pouch of fragrant herbs from her shoulder bag, and Kyra scooped the coins from her own. In moments, the trade had been made, and they both stored their prizes.

"A cup every morning," Velinda instructed. "But not while you carry."

Kyra's heart stuttered at that caution. "It will harm a child?" If it would, did she dare take it and risk injuring the babe before she realized she carried?

"Not at all, but why waste it? While you carry, there are no eggs released for you to react to."

She nodded, her body easing. "My thanks."

"It may take up to five days for full effectiveness, but it will work. You have my vow on Mag that it will."

The roar of a transport engine brought Kyra's head around. Captain Elez pulled up close, engaged the brake, and jumped out.

"Kyra Hir?"

She offered him a wan smile, suddenly as tired as she was supposed to pretend to be.

Jotem eased out of the transport, casting a fearful look at Elez. No doubt her guard had accused the young man of wrongdoing.

Kyra couldn't allow that. She stood and bypassed Elez to Jotem. Kyra pulled a gold coin from her bag and offered it to him.

The Sivrah looked at it, then met her eyes, seemingly confused.

"In thanks," she told him.

His gaze flicked to his sister, then back again. Jotem shook his head. "The silver you gave me was too kind. Your thanks is enough." He pulled the coin from his pocket and tried to offer it to her.

Kyra shook her head, at a loss. She couldn't take what was theirs. Even the five silver for the tea had been too little payment...an insult. She should have insisted on paying more.

Jotem hesitated, looked to his sister again, then returned to the transport and disappeared inside, taking the silver coin with him.

Kyra watched him go, at a loss to explain their reactions.

Velinda bowed her head and offered a whispered blessing on Kyra for her kindness. In the next heartbeat, she was mounting the stairs into the transport and closing the door behind her. The engine came to life, and they were in motion.

Elez's fingers cupped Kyra's elbow, and he guided her toward her own transport. "Should I call your woman healer?" he asked.

Kyra considered what was in her bag. "No. I believe I'll rest and partake of a tea."

* * * *

Steden ambled into the rooms he shared with Kyra, working the ties on his tunic in near-exhaustion.

It had taken hours, but they'd reversed the Oxykol in Alensa's system and saved her child. It would be her final child; there was no doubt about that. Though the woman produced highly-viable children, her body wouldn't take more of pregnancy and childbirth.

The room was still and dim, a soothing balm to his overtired body and mind. All he wanted was to divest himself of clothing and fall into bed. Even food and the bath could wait.

His tunic had been tossed over a chair when Kyra appeared beside him. She took over on his trousers, and Steden let his eyes drift shut. It wasn't until Kyra started pushing his trousers away...and her breasts nestled to his chest that he realized she was nude.

Normally, Kyra only humored his request for nudity when he was about. When he was gone, he knew, she wore clothing. His move to greet her came a moment too late.

"I have food for you."

Steden groaned. "Perfect." While seeking food out was beyond him, something readily available was acceptable. Toeing off his boots, he stepped out of the last of his clothing and headed for the table.

"The bed," Kyra corrected him.

He sank to the surface and stretched out, sighing in relief. Kyra collected the plate and fork, bringing a piece of roast kit to his mouth. Steden took it gratefully.

The first few bites passed in silence. Then Kyra started to speak.

"Did...did it turn out well?"

He nodded. "Yes. Alensa and her son will be fine, but he will be her last child."

Kyra darkened a notch, probably biting back the response that five children was more than adequate for any woman...or obsessing over the idea that they still hadn't conceived.

"And your day?"

She hesitated a moment, seemingly considering it. "Enjoyable enough, I suppose. I took a long walk in town. It was...refreshing."

Steden accepted another bite from her hand, wondering at the hesitation. He didn't wonder for long. Kyra's hand exploring his inner thigh and playing at the well of musk wiped the question from his mind.

"Kyra." He'd meant it as a question, but it came out a plea.

She set the plate aside and leaned over him, her breath warming his nipple, her tongue sampling his musk.

"Kyra, the musk is—"

"I know. I want you, Steden."

Fion, yes. If she wanted him, she'd have him...as often as her body would tolerate.

CHAPTER TWENTY-SEVEN

Zor 34, Ri 25-3017

Kyra sipped the last of her morning tea, staring at Steden, the hunger already growing in her. The Sivrah woman healer hadn't told her the tea would act as an aphrodisiac, as well as a curative, but perhaps it was beneficial that it did.

They'd made love twice the day before, the second late into the night. As a result, Steden was still sleeping, but he wouldn't be for long.

With the lessening of her response to completion, he'd encouraged her increased libido. There was little question that he'd let her entice him as often as she was willing to do so. The simmering arousal building in her reminded her that the tea would make her very receptive.

If my condition keeps improving, perhaps Steden will consider more than producing a child together. After all, his consideration and gentle touch had little to do with their sexual congress.

Her body preparing for him already, Kyra slipped into bed with Steden. He shifted, turning to her, wrapping one arm around her waist. She cupped his sac, kneading at him, seeking out the sensitive spot behind.

Steden moved minutely, a groan leaving his lips. "There. Touch there, Kyra."

A wicked little plan settled in her mind, and she used the other hand to bring his cock to her slit, rocking against it. "There, Steden," she teased.

His hands circled her waist. "Move your hands."

Kyra complied, and he tipped her away from him on the bed. In the next heartbeat, he was sheathed inside her, the crown of his cock lodged tight in the band.

Her body went wild, climaxing around him in great waves of sensation. Steden gasped, his hands tightening on her hips, forcing her tight to him. He roared, his cock erupting into her.

It was sublime. It was the perfect counterpoint to her continuing climax. His cock swelled, locking into her stim band, releasing her egg in a shower of overlapping sensation.

Kyra screamed, her entire body on fire for more of him. Her senses quieted slowly, amidst the quilt of panting breaths and wandering hands. She opened her eyes, sobering slightly at Steden's look of calculation.

"What is it?" she asked. Surely, she'd done something wrong, but Kyra couldn't imagine what it might be.

"Are you..."

It took a moment for his reasoning to clarify in her muddled mind. "No. I released an egg. I'm certain of it."

Steden smiled, his eyes glittering in something resembling amusement.

"I'm... I hesitate to say I'm cured, but—"

His smile widened further. "I knew it was possible," he imparted. "When the doctors could find no physiological cause, I knew it would be a matter of trust." His smile faltered. "You do trust me, don't you?"

"Implicitly."

But not enough to admit how I'm really doing this? A niggling of unease ate at her. Kyra pushed it away ruthlessly. What did it matter how she was doing this? As long as she could be the wife he deserved, the ends would justify the means.

His voice jerked her back to the present conversation, but not in time to catch what he'd said. "Pardon?"

"I said... Now, I really *must* contract with you."

Her heart ached at that comment. "If you don't want to—"

"Oh, I do. And I refuse to let any other man experience what I just did."

That wasn't much better.

Steden must have sensed her upset. His smile softened. "I love you, Kyra. I've loved you for years."

Her heart raced happily, and her cheeks heated. "You have?"

He nodded. "Will you contract with me?"

A laugh bubbled up. "A man who can make me climax that simply? Who else would I consider contracting with?"

CHAPTER TWENTY-EIGHT

Ite 22, Ri 25-3017

"Kyra," Jerrika called out. Steden's mother waved Kyra to the table, her smile wide and welcoming.

Steden rose, pulling Kyra's chair out and cupping her elbow with his hand to steady her as she sat. Kyra offered him a wan smile, settling her hand over the huge mound of their daughter. Steden leaned to press a kiss to her lips, then one to the babe, before taking his seat again.

"Are you well, Kyra?" Taven inquired. It had taken him four months after they contracted to stop calling her 'Kyra Hir.'

"A little tired, in the afternoons. The doctors have ordered a rest for me. I was taking one, regardless," she was quick to note.

"Good. Good." He looked toward the doorway. "Ah...the tea is here."

Eveleta set the tray on the table and started pouring and mixing in the sucre. She served Jerrika first, as a guest of the house. Had Kyra not been carrying, she would have served Taven next. As it was, she offered the second mug to Kyra.

She took it with a nod of thanks and drank down the first mouthful, gasping in surprise at the flavor.

"What is it?" Taven asked urgently. "Too hot?"

"More probably the babe kicking," Steden suggested. "She has quite the kick, when she's of a mind to."

Kyra stared into the mug, her mind rioting.

"What is it?" Jerrika asked. "Kyra, is something wrong?"

She looked up at Eveleta. "You took the tea from my rooms." How dare she! What was she thinking? Even if the tea wasn't so rare and precious, it was Kyra's.

The servant's brow furrowed. "Jerrika Laes asked for whiteroot tea. We were out in the kitchen, but I remembered—"

"This is a special mixture," Kyra interrupted her.

"My apologies. I will collect more at the market."

"You can't!" *How will I replace it?*

Kyra had been trying for months to find a Sivrah that knew the recipe. None claimed to know a Sivrah named Velinda, and none claimed knowledge of the tea she sought, even those reported to be woman healers. She only had half the bag left now...enough for two months after her eggs started dropping again.

Granted, that meant she had more than a year to find a source or purchase the recipe, but Kyra was at a loss. How could she find Velinda?

Steden's fingers stroked at her cheek. "Kyra? What is it? Why is the tea so important?"

She bit at her lower lip, considering how much to tell him. Would he be angry at the deception? She'd hoped to get more of the tea; she'd hoped she'd never have to tell him it was the tea and not herself that had caused the change.

"Kyra?"

"The tea..." She hesitated. "It was the tea."

"What was the tea?"

Kyra shot a glance at Taven, then looked back to Steden. "The tea...controls the reaction."

His confusion melted into amusement. "Kyra, that's not possible."

She pushed his hand away, miserable, disgusted with herself.

Taven cleared his throat. "Kyra, who told you that the tea would treat your...condition?"

She swallowed down a lump of fear, looking from face to face and settling on Steden. "A Sivrah woman healer," she admitted.

"A—" Steden's face darkened, and his jaw tightened. "A *what*?"

Kyra didn't answer him.

"What is in the tea?" Taven's voice was measured, a sure sign that he was fiercely angry.

She didn't answer, and her face heated.

"Kyra?" Steden prompted her.

"I don't know...precisely."

"And you took it?" Taven demanded.

Kyra cringed at the unspoken rebuke.

"Now, wait," Jerrika soothed her husband. "I can tell you at least seven of the ingredients by taste, and they are all perfectly—"

"But not all of them," he surmised.

"Well..." She sighed. "No. I probably can't identify all of them."

Taven offered a jerk of his head in agreement, then rose. "Eveleta, we will need the tea. Steden, I think it best to have both the tea and Kyra tested immediately."

Steden leaned toward her and kissed her cheek. "Yes. That's probably best."

* * * *

Steden sat at Kyra's bedside, his temper simmering. So far, all the tests of Kyra and their daughter had come back with encouraging news. Whatever the Sivrah had done to her, it seemed they hadn't poisoned her.

Still, there was no saying what the tea had done...yet.

In a sudden realization that Jerrika had sampled the tea before Kyra had, his father had insisted on a second clinic room for his mother, and both women had undergone a battery of tests. That was the only reason Taven wasn't hovering over Kyra, Steden was sure.

They were waiting on contacting Kyra's family. Steden had rationalized that there was no sense worrying them, until—*unless!*—they knew there was something in particular to worry them about.

"Are you very angry?" Kyra whispered. It was the first question of the sort she'd asked him.

"Were you really that desperate to have a child?"

"No." There was something unsaid.

"But?" he prompted her.

"I wasn't that desperate to have a child; implantation could have given me that. I *was* desperate for something else."

He met her gaze steadily, wincing at the mist of tears in her eyes. "And that was?"

"You." She swallowed what was probably a lump in her throat.

Forming a response to that was difficult. "You've always had me for the asking. Don't you know that?"

She shook her head, seemingly denying it.

Steden settled to the mattress beside her, taking her hand. "It's true, Kyra. On Mag's name."

"I couldn't be..."

"Be?"

"What you deserved in a wife," she complained.

"But you are. You always have been."

Whatever answer she meant to make was preempted by his father's bustling entry.

Steden took a calming breath in light of Taven's agitation. "What did the tests show?"

"There is nothing dangerous in the tea. Aside from a sand or two of olum per mug, it is inert. We can rest assured that the ladies are in no danger. Nor is your daughter."

Kyra launched against Steden's chest with a sob, fisting her hands in his tunic.

He enveloped her in his arms, barely breathing in the release of tension. "Thank Mag," he managed. "Thank Fion."

"I'll speak to General Neival," his father vowed.

Steden worked at that without return. "For?"

"We will find the Sivrah who sold Kyra the tea."

Kyra's voice came out trembling as hard as her body was. "B-but...it wasn't d-dangerous," she noted.

Steden didn't hesitate to answer. "She cheated you, Kyra."

She pushed away, shaking her head, her smile wide though tears had laid tracks down her cheeks. "No, she didn't. Don't you see?"

Steden didn't see. He didn't see, at all.

Kyra brushed a kiss against his lips. "She promised it would heal me."

"But it didn't," he argued. "It couldn't possibly have had an effect. Everything was inert."

"It didn't need to have a physical effect, Steden. Don't you see?"

He was starting to. "Kyra—"

"The tea did what it was supposed to do. I didn't react, because it was never a physical response. That's why the doctors couldn't cure it. I had to believe it would work. I had to want it to."

A smile pulled up at his lips. "You wanted it to work...for me?"

"Oh, yes."

"Then I owe the Sivrah woman a debt of thanks. I will assume she wishes to use it to escape punishment."

Kyra laughed aloud. "I would agree that's probably true."

EPIL⊕GUE

Wend 12, Ri 25-3018

"Majesty, I need a moment."

Jole glanced up at Panor, nodding his agreement. "I could use a pause in the workday."

Panor's jaw tightened in a manner that attested this would be no break.

"What is it?"

"We've intercepted a message you need to be aware of."

Jole noted the paper crumpled in his security chief's hand in apprehension. "Is that it?" He motioned to it.

"A likeness. The original is being tested...in an effort to trace one or both of the guilty parties."

"But the messenger—"

"Killed himself to avoid capture."

Jole took a calming breath. Whatever this was, it was serious. At a loss for words, he motioned for the paper.

Panor hesitated, then handed it over. He offered no explanation, letting Jole make his own determination.

The missive was rendered in an impeccable hand that spoke of training in protocol. The wording reinforced that belief.

Be prepared. We take the princess before her upcoming contract day. All depends on capturing her before that time.

"Eve," Jole managed, his breathing strangled. She and Jearsen had set the date for their celebration to coincide with the presentation of their second child.

"Or Gibril," Panor reminded him. "There is no way to be certain which princess it refers to."

"How did we come across this man?"

Panor's face tightened into a grimace. "The messenger stopped at an inn and...imbibed a bit overmuch. He started a fight with a young guardsman. When the other soldiers tried to arrest them both, the messenger killed himself. In searching for some clue as to who he was..."

"They found this?"

Panor nodded stiffly. "And immediately turned the matter over to the royal guard."

"Good." But it wasn't good. Either his daughter or his niece had been targeted by an unknown enemy for an unknown reason. There were far too many questions unanswered.

"May I suggest we place both princesses under heavy guard?"

Jole considered that. "Gibril won't stand for it...if she knows about it. And Michael..." His brother's reaction would be extreme, though there was no question he'd have to be warned. He tapped the missive against the desk, deep in thought. "Let me handle this."

"But—"

"I'll speak to Jearsen immediately. Assign a team of six additional guards to Eve, the best available. She is not to leave the palace without a squad...and a Len-damned good reason to do so."

He paused, working at the problem of his niece. "Send for Andrew. This is just the sort of challenge he likes."

To be Continued in...

Dⴰⵙⵤⵣⴱⵍⴻ Iⵕⴰⴳⴻ!

ABOUT THE AUTHOR

Brenna Lyons wears many hats, sometimes all on the same day: former president of EPIC, author of more than 100 published works, owner of Fireborn Publishing, columnist, special needs teacher, wife, mother...and member in good standing of more than 60 writing advocacy groups.

In her first ten years published in novel-length, she's won 3 EPIC e-Book Awards (out of 15 finalists) and finaled for 3 PEARLS (including one Honorable Mention, second to NY Times Bestseller Angela Knight), 2 CAPAS, and a Dream Realm Award. She's also taken Spinetingler's Book of the Year for 2007.

Brenna writes in 26 established worlds plus stand-alones, poetry, articles and essays. She's a bestseller in indie/e fantasy and horror, straight genre and cross-genres thereof. Brenna has been termed "one of the most deviant erotic minds in the publishing world...not for the weak." (Rachelle for Fallen Angels Reviews) Milieu-heavy dark work is practically Brenna's calling card, with or without the erotic content.

She teaches classes in everything from POV studies to advanced editing, networking to marketing. Brenna enjoys hearing from people who read her work and can be reached by e-mail.

Website: http://www.brennalyons.com/

Facebook: http://www.facebook.com/brenna.lyons

Email: brennalyons4168@live.com

Also by this Author

Hunter's Tales
Maher Men
The Blutjagdfrau Chronicles
Veriel's Tales I: Crossbearer Turned
Veriel's Tales II: Losing Regana

URBAN GRIMM
Catch Me, If You Can
Three Wishes
Temptation of Eve

WEREWOLF U
Werewolf U
Younger Daughter
Alpha Son
Never Alone
Her Christmas Wolves

ANGEL-WING SAGA
Sons of Heaven: Beldon
Sons of Heaven: Unexpected Mates
Daughters of Man: Prize Match
Daughters of Man: Claiming a Princess

COLOR OF LOVE
The Color of Love

KEGIN SERIES
Conquest
The Last of Fion's Daughters
Last Chance for Love
Rites of Mating
In Her Ladyship's Service
Matchmaker's Misery

KIELAN SERIES
The Lady's Lowborn Lover
Time Currents
Cubed

STAR MAGES
Written in the Stars
The Master's Lover

DAN AIDAN FAIRIES
Fairy Dreams
Monsters of Myth Anthology

XXAN WAR
Daahan Rising
Raashh Decisions

MYTHOS SERIES
The Punishment of Phoebus Apollo
Black Sail

IT'S ALL GREEK TO ME...
All's Fair...

SANCTUM
Dream Walk

GRELLAN WAR
With Great Power

BLOOD MAGES
Enslaved

CARSON COUSINS
All I Want for Christmas is You

FATES WAR
Fates Magic

Beyond the Veil
Mine for the Night
Once in a Blue Moon
Overtime Pay
Stay With Me
The Fire God's Woman

Nevermore
Bride Ball
Undead in Blue
Mama's Tales
Unexpected Daddy
We Shall Live Again
May the Best Man Win
Marked
And It Was Good
Monsters of Myth Anthology

Available from **Under The Moon**

Evil Overlords Union Issue #1 Anthology
Undead Embrace
"Playing Games" in *Forbidden Love: Bad Boys*
"Marked" in *Forbidden Love: Wicked Women*
"The Master's Lover" in *Forbidden Love: Sacred Bands*

Available from **Logical Lust**

"Mine for the Night" in *The Cougar Book* Anthology

Available from **Coming Together Charity Anthologies**

INSTINCT SERIES
"Foundling" in *Coming Together: Into the Light* Anthology

"Claim Mate" (available separately and as part of the
Coming Together: Against the Odds Anthology)
"The Fire God's Woman" in *Coming Together: Under Fire*
Anthology

Available **self-published**

Snapshots from a Poet's Life

AWARD-WINNING BOOKS

EPPIE/EPIC eBOOK AWARDS WINNERS
Coming Together: Against the Odds- 2010
Time Currents- 2010
Coming Together: Into the Light- 2011

EPPIE/EPIC eBOOK AWARDS FINALISTS
Fion's Daughter- 2004
Collected Poems: Book One- 2005 (now titled *Snapshots of a Poet's Life*)
Renegade's Run- 2005
Rites of Mating- 2006
All I Want for Christmas- 2006
Phaze in Verse- 2008
"The Fire God's Woman" in Coming Together: Under Fire- 2009
Three Wishes- 2010
Matchmaker's Misery- 2010
The Cougar Book- 2011
The Master's Lover- 2011
Bride Ball- 2011

DREAM REALM AWARDS FINALIST
Last Chance for Love- 2003

PEARL HONORABLE MENTION
Night Warriors- 2004

PEARL FINALISTS
Schente Night- 2003 (now included in *The Last of Fion's Daughters*)
König Cursebreakers- 2004 (now titled *Will of the Stone*)

JOYFULLY REVIEWED BEST BOOKS OF 2010
Written in the Stars- 2010

SPINETINGLER'S BOOK OF THE YEAR 2007

NOBODY: An Anthology of Dark Fiction- 2007 (Brenna's pieces of the anthology can be found in *Beyond the Veil*)

TRS's CAPA FINALISTS
Ultimate Warriors- 2004 (Brenna's portion is now available as *With Great Power*)
Written in the Stars

LOVE ROMANCE AND MORE CAFÉ BOOK OF THE YEAR RUNNER UP
Last Chance for Love- 2008

ROAD TO ROMANCE REVIEWERS' CHOICE AWARD
Prophecy: Revelations- 2004

LOVE ROMANCES REVIEWERS' CHOICE AWARD
Black Sail- 2003

ROMANCE JUNKIES BOOK CLUB STAFF PICK
TYGERS- 2003

FALLEN ANGELS ROMANCE RECOMMENDED READ
Devon's Price-2005 (now available in *Bearing Armen*)

JOYFULLY RECOMMENDED READ
Fairy Dreams- 2008
The Last of Fion's Daughters- 2009

TREBLE HEART FINALIST
Prophecy: Revelations- 2003

www.ingramcontent.com/pod-product-compliance
Lightning Source LLC
Chambersburg PA
CBHW050714180626
46814CB00002B/432